THE
OTHER
WAY ROUND...

THE
OTHER
WAY ROUND...

WHEN TRUTH IS STRANGER THAN FICTION

Dhaval Dange

Srishti
PUBLISHERS & DISTRIBUTORS

Srishti Publishers & Distributors
N-16, C. R. Park
New Delhi 110 019
srishtipublishers@gmail.com

First published by
Srishti Publishers & Distributors in 2012

Typeset by EGP at Srishti

DEDICATION

To
Aai & Baba

ACKNOWLEDGEMENTS

Throughout the process of writing this book since way back in March 2010, many individuals have taken time out to support and help me.

I would like to take this opportunity to thank my parents for always being there for me and for being the support that they are in every venture of mine. Thank you for tolerating my long nights on the computer along with the heavy music in the background while I wrote/edited the book. Also, thank you baba for inculcating good reading habits in me from the very start of my schooling by providing me with good books and stories that inspired me to be a storyteller.

I'd like to give a special thanks to Sagar Vairagkar for actively participating in the feedback and contributions for this book via our long mail trails and discussions. He was the very first person to have an idea of this book since its conceptualization and even before I typed a single character in the word document. Without his support, strong belief in me and motivation all together, this certainly would not have been possible.

I thank Soham Sabnis for designing and conceptualizing a

wonderful cover and working on it with the same passion and enthusiasm as me.

Thank you Srishti Publishers & Distributors for their inputs regarding the book as a whole. Without them, this transformation of book from mere word documents to a hard copy would not have been possible.

Last but not the least; I would like to thank all the readers that have taken a fraction of time out from their lives to give this book a read.

I'm sure I won't disappoint you and you'll enjoy every word of this.

Thank You.

"Faith is taking the first step even when you don't see the staircase."

THE PROLOGUE

Vishal Rajguru. At twenty-three years of age, his life would have been the same as any other average urban young boy's if it weren't for the unfortunate accident that resulted him going into a state of coma for the last few months. Now Vishal had just come back to consciousness. The room was silent, except for the slight spinning noise that the ceiling fan above his bed made. His head hurt a bit. He strained his eyes to see more. He didn't know for how many hours, days or even years he had been asleep. He scanned everything around him. It was a semi-private room in a hospital. Curtains were pulled over around the bed from all four sides, to give a certain level of privacy. Beside him, on a chair was another man, who was asleep, still in his sitting position, resting his head on the edge of hospital-bed on which Vishal lay motionless. Vishal could well see the analogue wrist-watch the man wore. 3.15 It read. By the intensity and shade of the lights that surrounded him, Vishal guessed it was past midnight and hence it must be A.M., 3.15 a.m. Within a couple of minutes, the sleeping man sensed the motion on the bed as he sprang up from his sleep.

"My God! You've opened your eyes! Vishal!" the man stood

up from his chair as he touched Vishal's forehead to check his temperature and asked, "So tell me, how are you feeling? Are you okay? You need something?"

"Errm fine." Vishal answered in a very feeble voice, "Where am I? What happened?"

"Don't worry, wait. Let me call the doctor first! I can't tell you how happy I am! God is great!" the man beside him ran for the doctor with excitement without answering either of Vishals' questions. Within a minute a doctor accompanied by a nurse came into the room as they began their examination while Vishal watched the happiness in the man's eyes and wondered what this was all about.

He didn't remember a thing; neither how he got into such a position, nor who the man beside him was.

About an hour later a team of two doctors along with the man who had been beside Vishal earlier stood before him. They all were smiling.

"Congratulations and welcome back." one of the doctors said.

Vishal was confused.

"Wh...what had happened? Where am I?" Vishal said, "I don't remember a thing."

"Don't worry. You'll be fine within a few days. In such cases there is initial loss of memory, but you will recover. You had met with an accident due to which you were in a state of coma. Right now all you need to do is rest and our only goal should be your speedy recovery."

"But.. I don't remember.."

"Vishal." the man spoke now, "Didn't you listen to what the doctor said? All that you need right now is rest and proper medication. Now that you are back, we have plenty of time to discuss other things! I'm so glad you're back!"

"For how long was I into coma? And what accident are you talking about?"

"Don't strain yourself. You were in coma for about 7 months now. And about the accident, it's good that you don't remember as you don't need to put pressure on your mind right now. You will remember everything eventually. And anyways this is no time to discuss it. We'll save that chat for later. Right now all I care about is how soon you can get on your feet and we can catch a weekend movie. Just like the old times." the man spoke again.

"7 months? That's quite a long time!" Vishal muttered, "But who are you?"

"I'm your college buddy, dude! You forgot that too? It's me man! Karan." the man finally introduced himself as Karan Thapar, Vishals' college friend as he came forward and gave Vishal a hug.

"Look at this." Karan said as he picked up a small photo-frame from beside the table. It had two young people smiling with arms around each other; two boys. One of the boys was Vishal himself and other was Karan.

Vishal had too many questions in his mind. He didn't remember a thing about his past, or even the 'accident' that had him end up in this situation. Even though the doctors said that he would eventually get back his memory, he couldn't wait any longer. All he prayed for was a miracle.

About two days passed.

Vishals' health was being monitored as usual on a regular basis now with a little extra care. Karan told him about their friendship from scratch and other incidents regarding them, in the hope that Vishal would remember something. Karan and Vishal talked for hours at a stretch and then the nurse would sometimes interrupt reminding Karan that Vishal needed some rest. Karan talked about the pranks Vishal and he pulled on some teachers and friends, about their favorite hangouts and the movies they caught up while the classes were bunked. Life seemed extremely normal like any other bunch of college kids, until this accident, of which Karan never spoke about. Vishal asked questions, Karan answered them. It was kind of an unspoken, unwritten drill. But the doctor was right; his memory wouldn't be back like magic and would take time. In some cases the memory was permanently lost. The doctors and Karan along with Vishal just hoped that he didn't fall into those rare cases.

Another day passed.

Vishal didn't remember or even relate to a single incident which Karan narrated to him till now. Vishal often asked Karan to tell him more about his personal past and the accident. But Karan avoided the questions as usual. The doctor too advised that it wasn't good to feed Vishal with too much of information at once. And the disturbing parts like the accident or any other heavy stuff could be kept aside for later. On asking about his own past and family in a broader view, Karan told him how Vishal and he were in their final year of pursuing their Masters in Computer Science degree. Vishal was from Nagpur, in Maharashtra. His parents lived in Nagpur while he had been in Pune for his education for the last two years. Karan had never told his parents about the accident until Vishal had slipped coma. The parents were worried and stayed beside Vishal for about two months straight, every single day. The doctors had no clue as to when Vishal would come out of coma and hence advised the parents to move on with their normal routines slowly and visit their son on regular basis as and when they wanted rather than spend their entire time staring at their motionless child. It was difficult for them. But life had to go on. Four months after the accident, Vishals' parents went back to resume their work in their hometown and visited their bedridden son every weekend. Then about a month later, they visited only once a month. They were slowly getting used to seeing their son less and had somehow accepted that they would never see him as he was before. After Vishal had come out of the coma, the first thing that struck Karan was to inform Vishal's parents about it.

They would be so happy to see their son recovering so soon from his deep sleep. But then Vishal still hadn't recovered his memory. And Karan decided to let them know about Vishal's recovery only after a week or two when Vishal would have recovered even more and hopefully his memory would be back too. The doctor said it could take a couple of weeks. Karan was optimistic that it would happen even before that. He wanted to tell Vishal's parents, share the joy and see for himself the happiness in their eyes that had been missing for the last so many months. But then something stopped him. He didn't want them to see their child with a confused look on his face as he didn't remember anything.

Yet another day passed.
Vishal was still clueless about his memory. The doctors had began to worry as even after four whole days of coming totally out of coma there was not even a single sign of his memory coming back. They found it strange as normally a person did not lose his entire memory in such cases but Vishal had lost it all, like a formatted hard-disk and they had no clue when it would be back. But in such cases it didn't take more than a month to regain one's memory. It's often regained in parts. Karan was just glad that at least Vishal was finally 'alive' and talking. He did not think much about the future. The future scared him with its 'ifs and buts'.

It was about 2 p.m. and the sun shined brightly outside the hospital building as Vishal sat on his bed reading a Readers' Digest after his lunch. Karan had gone to attend to some chores of his own. Vishal was now feeling more energized and fresh than he had been the day before. Soon the nurse entered the room for the daily mid-afternoon medicine. She greeted Vishal with a smile as she handed out the medicine to him.

"So how are you feeling now?" She asked.

"Fine." Vishal smiled.

He gulped in the medicine with a half a glass of water and then hesitantly asked the nurse, "Listen, I feel they're hiding something from me. How did this happen?"

"You mean the accident?" she asked.

"Yes."

"We'll I'm not supposed to say anything. And you don't stress yourself too. Just take rest as advised."

"No. I want to know. It's been bugging me ever since I woke up! It's frustrating that I can't remember a single thing and they wouldn't tell me about it!"

The nurse took a deep breath.

"See, I can't see you like this either. But let me tell you something. Don't go against them. They seem to be very powerful."

"They? Who?"

"Those people about whom you have written. They are in touch with the hospital authorities here. You'll never be told the truth. You'll be made to believe only what they say and nothing else."

"What are you talking about? What and when did I write?" Vishal tried hard to remember, but in vain.

"Oh God they didn't tell you that too" the nurse said, further increasing the stress on Vishal.

"What?"

"You were not in coma since the accident. You had a severe head injury during your accident, but then you were treated here for it. You were conscious for about four days after the accident and advised a month rest. You also had multiple fractures in your leg and a dislocated shoulder. But then to kill time, you began to write about some experience of yours during your stay in some camp or workshop you had attended earlier. Also, apparently, that is where you met with your 'accident'. You wrote relentlessly for three whole weeks and then you started to get fits on a regular basis. The doctors decided to operate on you as your brain MRI displayed a few blood clots. There was an emergency operation scheduled two days later and that is when you went into coma."

Vishal was stunned.

"These people told me I was in coma since the accident!" he said.

"It's a blessing in disguise for them that you don't remember anything!" the nurse said as she kept a close eye on her surroundings making sure no one was watching her.

"So these experiences of some camp or workshop, whatever, I had visited, where did I write those back then? And why is Karan hiding it from me? He never spoke or even mentioned any camp visit to me before."

"That I don't know. But you wrote in your laptop" The nurse said.

"Okay thanks a lot sister, just one more thing. Did anyone other than Karan visit me here?"

"Yes, your parents, a few of your college friends and that girl who's now gone to her hometown last week it seems, Delhi. Her name is Richa something, seems special. She cares so much about you." The nurse blushed as if Vishal had asked her out.

"You know a lot." Vishal said.

"Yes. Your friend Karan often gets bored and then bores me by telling your tales and stuff about your friends at times. But never discusses your camp visit or the accident."

"Was he there with me there too?"

"It seems so."

"And this accident, happened while I was there?"

"I don't know. When you and Karan were brought here, he was being treated by some other doctor. That girl, Richa was quite severely injured too with a cut on her face. They recovered within a week though. Minor issues as compared to you."

"She was here too? Injured? What did they say had happened to all three of us?" Vishal inquired further as one shock after another greeted him as the nurse narrated the truth.

"Yes all three of you. But I have no idea what happened or where it happened. When I asked about how the patients had sustained the injuries, I was told to shut up and do the job or leave."

'Why would they do that' Vishal thought. He somehow wanted to know what the secrecy was all about.

"Can you get me my laptop please?" he requested the nurse.

"Of course! In fact it's right under that medicine table on the shelf. Been there since the last time you wrote in it before the operation. You had completed your experience or story whatever is in it. You wanted it to be published for the world to know in case something happened to you during the operation."

"How do you know if I had completed it?"

"Because you had asked to postpone the operation date by two days as you didn't wanted to 'die' back then leaving it incomplete." She said.

"Okay thanks for the help." Vishal thanked her as she left.

Now Vishal's mind was cluttered with even more questions after the talk with the nurse. What was it that Karan and the doctors were hiding from him? Why was it somehow a blessing for them that he had lost his memory? What would go wrong if he got it back?

He then reached to the laptop on the shelf, booted it and the searched for anything that would be similar to what the nurse had told him that he was writing. Soon in 'My Documents' folder he found it, a folder named 'Personal'.

A list of word files. He had written a sort of personal diary in it.

This was the answer to all the questions that Karan had avoided answering. 'Reading this would reveal a lot of things' Vishal thought.

Vishal then double-clicked and the word file opened up in front of him on the laptop screen.

He now began reading his own story.

CHAPTER ONE

"Are you sure you want to get into this?" it was Neha eying me keenly even though she kind of knew what my answer would be. Also there was Karan right in front of me. All three of us sat in our college canteen having our usual iced-tea as we spoke, or let's say, argued.

"Yes." I responded.

"But our exam's only two months from now! You can't do this!" Karan was trying his best to convince me. I just responded by nodding my head.

"I know, but it's now or never. I really want to do this." I tried to convince them.

All the fuss was due to my decision of skipping the college for like two whole months and joining just before the theory exams, skipping the practical exams too (and of course appearing for them in next semester).

It was a big deal, especially for final year Masters in Computer Science student as these students are usually termed as 'nerds'. Their only world is them, the computer and now the internet. Some live on programming, some sleep on it, and some eat programs for a living. That's their daily dose of computers for living. This fact is true, but only for a few Computer Science students. The rest enjoy life as any other student does.

"Ok, so you skip the college. For like two months and then what?" Neha finally came to the point.

I was fully prepared for this now. I was just waiting for them to let me begin. I reached my pocket and brought out a cutting from a local newspaper.

"Have a look at this" I pointed to an advertisement.

"*A Way Around*" Karan read.

"Now what's that suppose to mean!" Neha was losing it.

"Read the entire thing." I tried to draw their attention to a small advertisement below the heading "*A Way Around* – Spiritual & Personality Development Program."

Neha and Karan both looked at me as if I had read out something in a language completely alien to them. It was the look that one would give a shopkeeper if he quoted a double the price for an item you wanted. I read further ignoring their glares "Re-claim your life. Learn to live. A unique and refreshing spiritual program to uplift, enlighten you. Feel the change. Remember no matter how big your problems are, there is always *A Way Around* them".

I stopped. Nobody spoke for about a minute after I read out the article. This was what I think they called pin-drop-silence. Even in the chaos around us in the canteen, I had experienced it.

"So you are telling both of us that you're going to skip college for like two months before the exams. Skip practical exams and stuff, for this? *A Way Around*!? I mean hello! What's into you suddenly?"

"Ok, now if you both calm down a bit, I would like to explain", I took a sip from my tea, "It's not at all about this workshop. It's not even that much about me joining the workshop."

"Then?" Neha interrupted.

There are times when guys don't like being interrupted, even by a girl. And this was one of those.

"Let me finish Neha!" I continued ignoring her *how-dare-you-cut-me-off* glare,

"Ok. So I had about a month back applied for a *Make Your Documentary* contest organized by Discovery Channel India. Professionals, non-professionals, almost about anyone and everyone are invited and welcome to submit their entries in the contest. My application was short listed amongst a few hundreds."

"Vishal my dear," it was Neha again with her usual sarcastic tone, "Could you like please give us only one shock at a time? I mean what's about this Documentary Contest now! *A Way Around* to some documentary contest? Tell us this was all a joke please!"

"No." I said calmly, "See, for the documentary contest all one has to do is submit his/her entries, which means, a documentary film of about 40 minutes."

"So why *A Way Around*?" this time it was Karan who was interrupting, but thankfully for valid question.

"Yes I'm coming to that," I continued, "See, forget India, there would be like hundreds of entries from a city, say Mumbai itself! Most of them would be on wildlife, bird watching or poverty in India based themes as they're usually favorites. On the other hand, I want to document something different. Maybe something as simple as the spiritual culture in an urban Indian city. India has long been the source of spiritual inspiration to the world and now we ourselves seek spirituality in various workshops held in urban India."

Neha finally managed to say something after my long explanation, "Vishy, You are nuts! I didn't get a word of what you said."

"I understand," Karan was now somewhat supportive, I thought, until he went on, "Basically you want to win the Discovery Channel's documentary contest by making a documentary film on the workshop called *A Way Around*. For what? Money?"

So now here's one of the few things I don't understand. Why do humans always sum up everything by economics? Why there's always an estimation of profits and losses rather than one's will or happiness or even just mere satisfaction of doing something? I kept my questions to myself and straightaway answered Karan.

"See," I cleared my throat, "See, I agree money is one of the major factors. There's like 5 lakhs of rupees as an award plus a scholarship in documentary film making in Chicago."

"So this is big, it seems," Karan interrupted.

"Yes," I cut him off before he went on, "Also, there are things that you do. Things you do for yourself, keeping money aside as a mere motivation. How many are things that you always wanted to do but never did because the person inside you held you back? The mere thought of what people might think about us has left many unhappy in their lives. Why do we always follow the society rules? You're a Computer or some Engineering student, so you shouldn't try your hand at Arts even if you getting an opportunity to explore it! I mean who sets these rules? Like there's a rule or something! We have one life and we should live it as we want to. When an opportunity comes to you to let you pursue your hobby for a while, why let it go just because traditionally and as per society rules it's unwise to even attempt it?"

"I see where you're going now," Neha said, "The usual 'rebellious' you! My god. And what about your parents? The College authorities, the permission you'll need to do all this all of a sudden in the middle of a semester?"

I smiled at both of them.

"Oh God, don't tell me you have already done that and NOW you're telling me this!" Neha had already got her answer.

"You won't get this. So let's drop further explanation" I said, "I just wanted to know what you felt about it, and unfortunately you're no different than others."

"I'm sorry." Karan was getting my point now, "I'm with you. Go for it if you think this is what you want. After all it's only for a couple of months. You can give your practical exams in the next semester, but can never pursue your dream, or get the opportunity if you lose it now."

I smiled at Karan gesturing a thank-you to him. I wanted to hug him. But was too lazy to stand up and reach him across the table.

"I'm not convinced, I still think it's really absurd, pointless," Neha was a tough one to convince, "But go ahead. As if you're going to drop your idea if I say no."

"True," I said, "But it's always better to know that people behind you actually support you when you're doing certain things and not cursing you for doing it. Ok, I want you to be happy too, let's try a trick. I will draw two chits, one with *A Way Around* written on it, and other with Not *A Way Around*. You pick one, whatever the outcome, I'll do it."

Neha just looked the other way. But I did what I had to. Tore parts of a paper from my notebook and made two chits.

"Now please choose one," I said with the two chits in my palms.

"Are you serious? Because every time we draw chits, I tend to win." Neha said as she picked one chit.

"Now open it and see. That's it, that's my decision," I said as I tore the remaining chit in my hand and threw it away.

Neha opened it. *A Way Around*.

"Okay then." Neha's voice was kind of squeaky now, "Good luck then, if this is what you want."

"Thanks Neha." I said as all three of us got up for our next class.

My job was done. I wondered if all important decisions in life could be taken so easily by drawing chits. It would help us save so much of time, thought and pointless debates!

After college just as we were leaving for our parking lot, Karan came to me yet again and hugged me, "Way to go mate."

"You already said that." I reminded him.

"Yes, but I mean it. Just tell me one thing."

"And what is that?" I asked.

"You had both of the chits with *A Way Around* written in it didn't you?"

I just smiled at him and said, "Wow, that didn't even strike my mind back then! If only you could have suggested me earlier. Thank god I was lucky Neha picked the right one."

No matter what I said, Karan knew me well enough.

He had his answer.

CHAPTER TWO

A Few Days Later...

"This is just insane!" Karan whispered to me as we stood in the queue at the *A Way Around* entrance, "Still can't believe I'm in this with you."

"Well no one forced you to do so." I said calmly. It is kind of funny and annoying too when a person actually makes his decisions and blames others for it.

Giving me a cold look which I effortlessly ignored, Karan stood silently in front of me now saying nothing. I glanced around.

And there I was, with Karan showing his 'support' for me by following my footsteps and joining me in the documentary adventure, needless to say skipping the exams. We were at the '*A Way Around*' 14 day workshop in Lonavala, a place near Pune, Maharashtra.

We were 15th or 16th in the queue of like 40 people attending the workshop.

There was a checking counter right outside the workshop-bungalow where we all had to deposit our cash, mobiles and other 'materialistic or digital distractions' as they called it. If anyone asked me, I would never term any piece of technology as 'a distraction'. But rules are rules. They had stated it earlier in their norms; we had accepted it, signed the form and now had to follow it.

In front of me stood Karan my friend, philosopher and as I tease him at times misguide too. In front of him was a foreign couple chatting with each other. Behind me stood an uncle, in his early fifties or possibly late forties. The line moved at a snail's pace. And I considered it a good enough opportunity to start making friends. I turned back to greet the uncle behind me.

"Hi sir, Vishal."

"Hey young boy," he greeted me putting his right hand forward, "I'm Rajnish Khurana. Nice to meet you."

I smiled and greeted him too. Found out he was older than he looked, age-wise. Retired just a year ago and with plenty of time in hand, uncle Khurana was just another first-timer for this '*A Way Around*' workshop. His wife had passed about a couple of years ago. His name somehow had a resemblance to the 1970s *Bollywood* movie villains.

He asked me about my whereabouts and the usual stuff like what I study, what brought me here etc.

"So Computer Science ha?" I knew this would come from the uncle, "What are you doing here then?"

"Just like that uncle." I replied politely though I knew I wasn't making much sense to him but still it was far better than doing the entire explanation session I had done with Karan and Neha, "Like there's a rule or something! That a computer student can't attend a workshop."

"No of course not." uncle forced a smile, "It's only that you're not even Arts or Commerce student. That, I would have understood."

"So?" I was always surprised with this mindset of people. Why do people always think that students pursuing Arts/Commerce have fewer challenges and hence have the right to enjoy or *do-*

whatever-they-want as their birth-right?

We spoke for about a couple of minutes more as the line inched further. I was interrupted by Karan as he mentioned my name to someone, "And here's my friend, Vishal."

I extended my hand to the foreigner standing in front of Karan "I'm Thomas," he said, "And this is my fiancée Stacy." Stacy then extended her hand. They looked a perfect couple. Thomas was well built brown haired, broad jawed and Stacy was short as compared to him but a beautiful blonde.

Apparently they were here to 'explore' India all the way from Australia. I wondered how they planned to achieve their goal in *A Way Around* workshop. But that was left to them for now; since when did I tend to go on bothering about strangers for no reason like many do. And then a few minutes of chat with Thomas and Stacy came our turn at the counter.

A bald man of about 40 something was behind the desk.

"Bags here sir." he said.

We obeyed. Karan and I kept our sacks on the table.

"Welcome to *A Way Around,*" he greeted us with a smile so perfect and welcoming that I guess he practiced it in front of mirror every day, "Hope you have a good time here, I'm Krishna."

"Nice to meet you," I extended my hand, "I'm Arjuna and here's my bro Bhima"

Krishna widened his eyes as he gave us a puzzled look.

"Just kidding, sorry," I said as Karan made his *stop-it-please-that-was-lame* look, "I'm Vishal and this is Karan" I then corrected myself.

"Sir, I'm sure you know you have to leave all your digital distractions in your lockers. A strict NO for them while the workshop is on." Krishna was speaking officially now, using his *no-more-messing-up-with-me* look. There's always something strange about people's looks that they give while communicating. It says it all. Just a look is enough. No wonder it's said that pictures speak a thousand words. I would say facial expressions speak a million.

"Yes, sure." Karan obliged as he started scanning his bag for his 'digital-distractions'.

"iPod?" Karan asked as he held the device which he had just removed from his sack.

Krishna gave a 'No' signal. Karan handed over the iPod, he wasn't happy now.

"It's only a matter of 14 days man, chill." I consoled Karan, which anyways wasn't of much help.

While everything was being sorted out at the counter, I glanced around. There were people, all kinds of them. Friends in their 20s or 30s to retired oldies, to single travelers come here to seek another experience of some kind.

"Your handy-cam please," Krishna pointed out at the Sony handy-cam in my hand.

I was surprised now; I had already sorted this issue while registering with *A Way Around*. They knew about my documentary plans and with some conditions and restrictions which I obeyed to, they had no complaints.

"See, I think there's some mistake." I explained, "I've taken a special permission for this. I'm here on a documentary agenda. Also have the clearance of the authorities. You may ask them"

"I'm sorry, but rules are rules sir," Krishna said, "I am not aware of any such concession given to any of the student here. Do you have a letter or anything of that sort that allows you to keep your digital distraction with you?"

"Well I was told that I would get a special ID or letter of some sort once I get here"

"Okay then step aside sir." Krishna pushed aside my sack from the table as he spoke further, "Please contact Ms. Puja Kumar for further assistance, and she might have some idea about your situation."

I wondered if this was due my bad attempt to rope in the Mahabharata characters into my joke. I was left with no choice but to follow further instructions as per Krishna. Later I was told to visit the office at the back of the building where I would find Puja, the in-charge of the registrations and regulations stuff. I moved away from the line, asked Karan to move on with his formalities as I dealt with my current situation.

I walked through the front lawn of the *bungalow* towards the entrance and took a left in order to reach the back to the office area.

The office was a medium sized room with a partially blurred glass door, which gave an idea that there were already two people inside; two women, to be precise. One was seated in her arm chair, which of course would be the Ms. Puja I was looking for, while the other one was with her bag around her shoulder talking to Puja. The door wasn't closed properly which conveniently let out the not-so-pleasant conversation that was happening inside.

"See it's just a matter of a signature, I forgot ma'm, please understand." the girl with the bag was pleading.

"Ms. Richa Rao, my dear", Ms. Puja on her chair continued as she waved some documents in her hand towards the girl with the bag whom she called Richa, "See it's not a matter of a mere signature. The thing is, either you get your guardian's signature on all these documents or we will have to call them and ask them to come here and verify that you've come here with their permission. Rules are rules."

Now I was getting it. That Richa girl, had apparently 'forgotten' to get the signature of her guardians on like 'every' single form of the registration documents. Weird. Obviously as per the institute's program policy, people below 24 years of age required authority or consensus of their guardians to participate in *A Way Around* workshop.

I found it weird for an independent organization to stick to an age limit for no rhyme or reason. But found it even weirder for the girl who came with unfinished documents hoping to be still taken in. The argument had been going for about ten minutes now. Also, it was quite clear that the girl wasn't willing to give her parents or any other guardians' number to the authorities. She said that they hadn't agreed to her participating in the program and the fact that a call from here to get them just to verify or sign a document in would rage them even more. Surely I was missing something here. But the gist of the conversation made one thing clear. A girl needed help and the woman on the chair with authority wasn't providing any.

"Hello?" I was distracted with the woman on the chair calling out for me, "Who's there? Please come in."

Ms. Puja had noticed me waiting outside for like ten minutes. I pushed the glass door as I entered.

As I entered, a nice fragrance welcomed me. The nice floral fragrance coming from the girl with bag welcomed me. I looked at her, Richa. I smiled, she smiled back.

'*Beautiful*' was the only word that came to my mind. Though I didn't say it out a loud, at least I think I didn't. Richa was a nice looking girl with that perfect girl-next-door looks. Partially brown coloured black hair, sharp features with eyes so sharp that might just cut you into half merely by their look. Not that I hadn't seen anyone as beautiful as her, but there's something that instantly connected or attracted you about a person. The X-factor perhaps as some reality-show would call it.

"Yes?" it was Ms. Puja now, interrupting my thoughts.

"Good morning ma'm." I greeted her like a good boy explaining my situation to her.

"Okay, I guess it's some kind of miscommunication from our side." Puja admitted, "Will be sorted in no time, don't worry. You'll be getting a special ID card which you must display if any of the staff asks you for your digital distraction or isn't allowing you to film at times."

"Thanks a lot." I was relieved.

"But you do know we have a certain restrictions here, you'll be allowed to film only parts of our sessions as and when allowed by the authorities."

"Absolutely ma'm." I obliged.

"Also, in the end, your entire film or documentary whatever you're making will be reviewed and edited by our authorities if required" She reminded me of my special contract with the organization.

"Yes, of course" I was okay with it.

"Good, you may go now, I'll make a call and you'll be allowed in for further processing." she said picking up her phone as she dialed some numbers.

I turned around to leave. Richa smiled again as she still stood there with her forms in her hand. I wanted to help her in some way or the other, I didn't know why.

And then suddenly something struck me; an idea that would be helpful to her perhaps.

"Hey-hi Richa! How have you been?" I screamed out pretending like I've noticed her just then. This stupid plan of mine if it worked would either help her, or might lead to a stage where I would need help.

Richa gave me a surprised look, thankfully didn't say out anything though. From the corner of my eye I noticed Ms. Puja was puzzled too.

I quickly gave Richa a '*just-play-with-it*' kind of look.

"Oh hi.. you…" Richa picked up from where I left. Obviously, she was looking for something to start with.

"Forgot me didn't you! And you always said 'Vishal you have such a small memory chip in your head'!" I quickly wrapped and presented my name to Richa in my sentence without letting Ms. Puja know that she was going to be outplayed.

Ms. Richa went two steps further, "You haven't changed a bit Vishu!" she said mockingly as she hit me with the document roll on my arm. 'Whoa' I thought, 'smart!'

This girl sure had brains and was playing the game better than me now.

"So, what's the deal? What's wrong?" I enquired even though I knew what it was all about.

"Arey see na," Richa began as if I really was her childhood buddy or something, "I forgot to get my mom-dad's signature on these forms and for such a little thing these people want at least one of my parents to come here and tell to them that they're okay with me attending this seminar! Can you believe it?"

"Is that so?" I turned to Ms. Puja now.

"Firstly, it's none of your business." Puja replied to the nonsense happening out there, "And secondly, as an organization, we require someone to take an authority of a person attending our workshop for various reasons that you need not know."

That was harsh, but the truth. It was indeed none of mine or Richa's business or concern as to why certain forms need to be filled according to certain rules. But that's how the world moves on smoothly doesn't it.

"Okay all you need is someone to take authority right?" I asked further stating the obvious, "Is it okay if I sign the docs as her guardian, big deal?"

"Okay boy, enough. Your problem is solved, you may go." Puja was not entertaining us any more now, "Plus, this isn't a joke. We don't allow strangers to take authorities of each others as guardians."

"Ma'm" I interrupted her, "See, firstly we aren't strangers as you might have seen. We have known each other since like the 8th grade and our dads are good buddies too. After 10th we relocated hence lost touch. Her parents won't mind even if I sign here as her care-taker. Also, if by any means she wanted to trick you into something, she would've faked up her parent's signature. But she didn't do it, right?"

Now Puja was listening. Actually listening. God bless those random made up stories and un-interrupted ability of one to say false things and make up even more stories that seem true when said confidently. It's a blessing in disguise.

"Also, what does a guardian mean? Just a person who can take guard of you. Takes good care of you right?" I continued, "And I see nothing wrong if one is willing to take responsibility for his or her friend. You have verified my details, she's my friend, and I'm ready to take her responsibility. Hold me accountable if anything goes wrong."

"I see." Ms Puja now seemed quite convinced, "For now, we'll allow her to attend, though we will run our verification process as and when we want, just so you know. It's a protocol."

"No issues." Richa quickly chipped in.

I signed on the documents for Richa and within the next five minutes we were out of the workshop office. Though it wasn't over yet, but we had managed to hold off the mess for some time. Our problems were solved, at least temporarily, and moreover I had earned a beautiful friend.

"So you know my name *haan*? What are you, a stalker?" Richa said eying me as we walked through the lawn towards the front side of the building now.

"Is that how you kids say 'thank you' now-a-days? But anyways, I heard your name as she was yelling at you while I was waiting for my turn to be yelled at." I fought back politely.

"I didn't mean to say it in a bad way but thank you man." Richa giggled.

"So what's with this forgetting signatures and incomplete forms thing about?" I was curious as I was sure this wasn't as simple and innocent as it looked to be.

"Hold it boy," Richa stopped, "That I would like to keep to myself for now. Keep walking, Ms Puja can still see us from her half open glass door."

I obeyed. We walked together for like the next two-three minutes and then split-up as we joined different registration lines for further formalities to be completed, which included the handing over the locker keys to store our wallets, mobiles and other stuff.

The remaining part of the day went in getting acquainted with the teachers in the workshop, exploring the place. We were handed out the special 'workshop T-shirt' which had their symbol a *ying-yang* type of circle but with arrows.

The green colored T-shirt was quite a decent piece of fashion work, just like something one would wear for an evening walk or something, basically comfortable. Apparently, they had a different color for every day of the week. Neat and thoughtful.

✳ ✳ ✳

"So, everything sorted out?" Karan was asking me regarding the confusion we had about an hour ago with Krishna.

"Yes, they've allowed me with my digital distractions." I replied with a smile.

"Good."

Then I saw Richa from the corner of my eye, trying to fit something in her locker. I smiled again.

Clearly there was something in her that had attracted me to her the moment I saw her. I was yet to find out what, or maybe I would never even find out.

You cannot actually and always say why some emotions come to you, can you?

CHAPTER THREE

Day 1
6.20 a.m.

It was day one at the *A Way Around* camp. It was my first 'Dear Diary' moment for the documentary. I got up from my bed and peeped out of the window. It was pretty dark outside. It was the chilling winters and hence the sun was not allowed to show up until like about 6.30am or so in this part of the world. I then glanced at the table that was just near my head to check the time in my cell-phone. Not surprisingly, it wasn't there as everyday it would have been. For two main reasons. One, It was not my home and my room where I had slept last night and secondly, more than just a cell-phone, it was now a 'digital distraction' and hence was in the locker; safe and sound and useless.

'Will get used to this soon' I thought. And then was the big surprise. Karan wasn't there. 'He's already up?' was my first thought.

But then I saw Karan, with an even bigger surprise. It didn't take me long to realize that he wasn't only up early in the morning, but ready too!

"Why didn't you wake me up?" I was annoyed or rather

somewhat jealous of being woken up all by myself only to find out that Karan was up earlier.

"Good question." Karan was teasing me now, "Well there's only one bathroom per room, remember?" And on second thoughts he was right too. Two people shared a room with two beds, a common table, a small wardrobe and a common toilet. There was no point in both getting up at the same time and quarrelling over who used it first. At least I get extra sleep. Good.

"And see," I said, "Now that you're here, something good's happening. I mean you got up early! Now you know what an early morning looks like."

"Yeah yeah." Karan ignored my comment as he was in front of the mirror that hung to the wall adjusting his hair as if he was going to walk the ramp any moment now. I watched him set the hair on his forehead. This Shah Rukh Khan was ready for his shoot now.

I got up to get ready now as I could see the sun slowly taking over the darkness outside. I was just glad that Karan wasn't cribbing and the day felt fresh and wonderful to start my documenting.

So it was about 7a.m now. I stood on one corner of the lawn with my handy-cam recording a minute or two of the on-going yoga session. I was told I was allowed to record a few bits and pieces of all the sessions and activities but I had to join as soon as I was done with it. Of course I hated the part that the editing rights were with the management of *A Way Around* more than me.

'Will scan and pan the entire lawn and this will be like the opening of the documentary with the narration in the background' I was thinking. There were people in their morning slim-fit suits. Quite strange but not-so-slim people's outfits for the yoga session were also called slim-fits.

"And now we do the *Pranayam*", the instructor announced, "This one is a breathing exercise that is essential for..." I lost track of what he was saying due to a slight disturbance. Karan was actually yawning at the yoga session; this must have been the second time that I noticed it. 'Will have to edit it out from the recording tape if at all it's being caught in the frame' I made a mental note, ' Yawning people at the opening scene of the documentary, not good'. And then something on the handy-cam screen caught my attention. Yes, Ms. Richa Rao, there she was, so sincerely and elegantly doing her yoga. 'Now this is some opening credits stuff.' I thought to myself.

I still wondered what I actually liked about here. It was not that she was the most beautiful face I had ever seen but then one might never know. Maybe it was her hair, her eyes, maybe it was just her. It surprised you at times to know that how much less you know about yourself.

"Sir," the instructor called me, "You may want to join now".

I kept aside the handy-cam and joined the rest of the session. Now it might look beautiful from a distance, but let me tell you, yoga is not a piece of cake. You need to be as flexible as a snake when you're at it.

Only one thing good about the current session was that the instructor was aware of this fact and not-too-hard *asanas* were being practiced.

After about thirty minutes of the yoga sessions, it was time for relaxing and to refresh oneself for about ten minutes or so, and then everyone headed towards breakfast. Breakfast was arranged in the lawn itself. There was *Poha, Upma* and *idli-sambar. Poha* was my instant choice.

As everyone rushed towards the stall Karan came beside me, "Man I'm sleepy." and he yawned, again.

"Yeah I could see that!" I responded. Then I saw Richa, in the other line, opting for *Upma*.

'So *Upma* it is' I thought. "Please excuse me, I'm heading for *Upma*", I excused myself from Karan.

"Hey, you wanted *pohe* no?" Karan was surprised by my

sudden change of decision.

"Yeah right," I said as I was making my way towards the *Upma* line, "I 'wanted' it. Now I 'want' *Upma*."

Thankfully, Richa was the last person in the queue and I could join her making her the second-last person in the line now.

"Hey hi, good morning!" I blurted out, not sure what to say, "So *Upma* ha?"

"Ya", Richa said as she turned back to look at me, "so from *Poha* to *Upma* ha?"

Okay so she was observing me. She knew I had changed my loyalties at breakfast.

"Nothing like that, it's just that this line was little shorter than that one so..." I trailed off as we inched further for our turn. There are things that you plan in your head to say to a person when you are kind of attracted and want to make the best first impression, but when the actual time comes, that just doesn't happen. You lose your wit, humor and sense of all that you want to say.

"So guardian ha? Long lost friend?" Richa winked at me interrupting my thought process and referring to my 'heroism' that I showed yesterday.

"What do you mean? You needed help, so I offered it." I answered.

"No, that's okay I mean," she went on "But you could have mentioned you are my cousin or something right? A friend straight away, smart ha, not that I mind or anything." She was giggling.

I wasn't sure if she was flirting or asking me to stay away. I couldn't make anything out from her tone.

"See, are you saying indirectly that I helped you only because you're a girl and made it a good enough reason for me to hit on you? Wow!" I was furious now with that sudden assumption of hers, "If that's the case, I'm sorry I offered help."

"Ohh boy, don't misunderstand me. I was just pulling your

leg!" She was giggling even more now.

I guess she had found her source of entertainment in me while she was to kill her time in the *Upma* queue.

"And yeah, I could have said I'm your cousin or something, but then that would have complicated matters, for then, it would be expected of us to know each other very well!" I finished.

We inched forward further in the queue. She turned away from me now.

'Wow', I thought, 'this is just what I did not want right now! Of course she was joking and here I went all hyper with my stupid explanation!'

It's best that you keep quiet when you don't know what to say. So I did just that.

For the next one minute or so we observed an awkward silence. I decided to take the initiative to break the ice, "Umm… so what you having? *Upma*?"

"No. I'm having *Biryani*."

"What?"

"Isn't this a queue for *Upma*?" She quipped.

'Damn, there you go again' I thought, 'that was quite stupid Vishal, when will you learn!' I told myself.

We moved further as it was Richa's turn to have the *Upma*. She half-filled her plate with *Upma* and moved away. I did the same. I glanced at the adjacent *Poha* line. Karan's turn was yet to come. I scanned the open lawn for a free chair to sit and enjoy the breakfast. The *Upma* smelt good and had a nice aroma coming out make me want to have it all at once. Then I spotted an empty chair, and another one beside it. I hurriedly walked up to it and sat down. I reserved the other chair for Karan by pulling it near to me, just so that people know that this one was to be soon occupied.

Just when I started digging into the *Upma*, I noticed someone pull the chair beside me that I had reserved for Karan.

"May I?" a female voice was asking if the chair could be

taken.

I looked up from my plate, it was Richa. I swallowed my first bite of the breakfast without even tasting it properly, "Of course, but actually my friend is coming so I had..."

Before I had even completed my sentence, Richa had decided to help herself and sat there.

"So, tell me," Richa was smiling and I wasn't sure if it was in a good way or not, "What's your story?"

"Sorry?" I was surprised and not sure what this was all about.

"Chillax dude," she said, "You seem to be rather a nice person and you've helped me. It's just that you tend to be a little nervous, I don't know why. I'm just trying to make a new friend here and given that you're my 'guardian' now. I'm not a bad person too." She giggled again.

Wow, this girl had observed a hell of a lot about me in the short meet of ours, I realized. As she had mentioned the word 'guardian', I thought she was trying to be around me just so that the workshop authorities (if they're spying) would think that we really knew each other.

"Okay so you playing the guardian card now, so that they don't know about the lie ha? Well, no one's watching, you can relax." I started digging into my *Upma* again.

"Dude," she said again, "What's your problem?"

"I'm sorry," I looked up, "I do mess up sometimes, thought you were here to pull my leg again."

I extended my hand further for a shake "Hi, Vishal."

She shook hands with me; we shared smiles, genuine ones for the first time. I loved her smile. This was the first time I had noticed something beautiful about her other than her eyes. And her hair.

"So..." She said.

"So?" I came back from my thoughts.

"I mean you haven't answered me yet," she said as she started playing with her breakfast with the spoon.

"Oh, my story." I said taking another bite, "There's nothing much to say as such. I'm Vishal Rajguru from Pune, originally from Nagpur but currently pursuing Post-graduation from Pune."

"I see," She said as she questioned further, "and what brings you here? That too with your handy-cam! I mean you're the only person who is allowed to carry his digital distraction along here!"

Both of us laughed. I went on to explain 'my story' further.

"Boy you're good!" she said.

I really felt good now, for no reason. Or perhaps because she had said it.

"Your turn now." I asked her.

"Ummm.. What you want to know?" She asked.

"Anything," I said, even though I wanted to say 'Everything'.

"Okay, see," She began "Basically a Delhi girl, I mean born and brought up in Delhi but always on the move. Daddy has business in a couple of cities around India including Mumbai, Chennai and Ahmedabad."

'Whoa' I thought. She went further, "Also, I have run away from the family a couple of months or so back...."

"What?" I wasn't sure if I heard it right.

"Yeah" she continued, "My family has been kind of like *get married and settle down* stuff since last year or so. I tried convincing them that I wanted to pursue my passion for photography for a year or two. But they wouldn't listen."

"Bravo!" I said thinking, 'I wouldn't do that. Welcome to the 21st century.'

"So why don't you tell them that you will of course marry, but you need time."

"You think I didn't try?"

I nodded. Parents can be tough to manage at times. I had my own experiences while making them agree to my 'documentary mission' as well. In Richa's case, it was marriage; even more hard.

"So, got any ideas that I could use?" She asked as she had a bite from her breakfast.

"Ideas? Runaway ideas?" I asked.

"No, Idea in the sense the ones that I could use to postpone my marriage or ask them to just stop thinking about it for the time being?"

"Yes. Tell them child marriages are not legal here." I answered.

She laughed, I laughed too. It was a lame joke, but didn't matter, my audience was happy.

"So now that you're here, on your own your usual run-away from home?" I asked further.

"Yeah you can say that, but this is not the first time I've run away. Last time I ran away to Goa for like a week or two. My demands are often met when I return home after a runaway vacation."

"You are one spoilt girl!" I said, "I like that."

She gave another smile or maybe a mild laugh if there's anything like that.

"So, you opted to run away here all the way from Delhi? My my" I was surprised.

"Naah." she corrected, "We have been our Mumbai house for the last eight months or so, I came from Mumbai."

We had finished our breakfast, when I saw Karan walking towards me. I waved at him.

He saw me, then glanced at Richa and gave me *Oh-so-there-you-are* look. I ignored it.

"Ohh , I see your friend's here." Richa said as she got up, "We'll catch up later."

"Yeah, but you can stay." I told her, "He'll join us."

"Naah, anyways our breakfast time is about to get over. Will meet your friend later." and she smiled again as she walked away.

"Aye friend!" It was Karan now with his plate of *Poha* in his hand, "I see what's happening now." he was kind of in the teasing mode now.

"Actually this seat was reserved for you." I confessed.

"Yeah right." Karan said as he sat beside in the chair vacated by Richa, "And she what, like barged in just like that and occupied it?"

"I see, now you pull my leg too." I said ignoring Karan.

"Me too? You mean she too pulled your leg did she!" Karan wasn't going to stop now. He had found perfect entertainment, the next best thing to entertain himself after his iPod. I just got up to walk away for some fresh air.

"Yeah go now", Karan spoke on, "So where did you tell her to wait for you now that you've got an excuse to walk away? Admit it; you've got a crush on her no?"

I smiled at him in *I'm-just-going-to-ignore-your-comment* way.

Friends! They'll be always there for you, in love and war and sometimes little teeny-tiny crushes too.

CHAPTER FOUR

Day 2

I adjusted my Sony handy-cam on its tripod. A few changes in the setting, a final look at the view that I would get from where the camera was placed and I was ready.

"Shall we start, Sir?" I asked Mr. Rathod. He replied with a nod sitting in his armchair.

It was day 2 at the camp. I had acquired special permission to interview a few of the staff members of the workshop for my documentary and what other good way to start than the founder and Dean of *A Way Around* himself!

Ravi Rathod was in his late fifties but looked fortyish and was a stout man. The thick moustache made him look rather tough even though people said he was the most friendly and easy going person in the camp. Now how many Deans do you expect to be easy going? One hell of a rarity isn't it?

"How much time will this take?" it was Rathod's P.A. standing beside his chair, Kaushal Prajapati. He gave me strange vibes and his rough voice added arrogance to his tone even more. Unlike the Dean, he was a tall man with average but grumpy looks. He looked like one of those P.T. instructors in school who looked as if they'll chew up their students if angry. He had his hair dyed with some pitch black colour which made it look even more obvious that he 'had' white hair deep inside.

"Just about 20-25minutes, Sir." I answered politely.

"Okay, make it fast."

The setup was ready, I was finally going to interview the founder and Dean of the workshop, followed by some other people too in the coming few days. Some perfect documentary stuff was due on its course (At least that's what I thought back then).

I made myself comfortable in front of him.

"So, let's start from the beginning." I cleared my throat, "How and where did all this start? *A Way Around*, I mean."

Rathod gave a smile, sat up straight in his chair, "Hmm, it was about 28 years ago that this actually happened," he stared at the ceiling kind of trying to re-create his era as he continued, "But you know what, I give the credit of this to every single thing that happened to me since my childhood. I was a complete failure since my childhood. I never liked studies, or let's say I wasn't made for traditional education. Due to family pressure and stuff I made it through school, my college life was worst. I was totally spoilt by then. I had been in the wrong circle of friends, bunked classes and faked mark sheets at home. It was quite clear by then that even graduation was certainly not my cup of tea.

My dad was a tough guy. Just at the age of 23, I was given two simple choices. Either I must pursue my education properly and find a decent job like many of his friends' sons or daughters did, or leave the house. For me, the second one was easier."

Rathod then paused for a moment. I decided not to interrupt.

"I had a friend who stayed in a hostel in Mumbai, close to where we lived." Rathod continued, "For a couple of days I managed to stay there without letting anyone know. But eventually we were caught and were expelled from there, thus making me a nomad. Now there were two of us, both homeless.

We went to the railway station and decided to get into whichever long distance train came first, and we did so. We wanted God to choose where we would go from here. And he did. After hours and hours of train journey and switching a couple of trains on random stations, guess where we landed."

I did not say anything. He went ahead with his story.

"*Varanasi*. The land of God as they say. There we wandered for days. Roaming about like nomads and eating *Prashad* from various temples to fill our stomachs, until we found a small unit of holy sages with their own little *Ashram* or training school as you may call it. The *Ashram* consisted of about a 50-60 devotees many of whom were foreigners. Initially everything seemed very vague, bizarre and unreal. The way people were mesmerized by the chants and the teachings was new to us. It was a new world, one whole different world you see. We saw people evolve, we saw ourselves evolve over a period of time. The city began gulping us and left us in a trance quite often. There was something unusual in that place, that environment, which brought you closer to god, closer to yourself. The city was in a trance all by itself, and so were the people. It somehow taught us in due course of time that most of the petty things we worried about in our lives did not really matter. We were changing, for good. In the midst of all of these, my friends' parents somehow found out about our whereabouts. He was taken away. I stayed. About 3-4 years passed by and I got the news of my parents' death in a bus accident. I didn't care, didn't feel a thing somehow, I was stronger and nearer to God now. This made me realize, that problems and situations like these break so many of our people and hence they came here for peace and getting enlightenment. Then it struck me. Life was all about ups and downs like these and everyone had them. Everyone had their own share of good and bad, happiness and sorrows in their lives, but all they needed was a place to let it out sometimes. Not everyone could handle their sorrows. I wanted to make it easy for people to access such outlets to enlightenment or relaxation of body and soul, with a difference. Not everyone knew of *Varanasi*, nor everyone who needed spiritual, mental or emotional strength came here. So what could I do? If people couldn't access enlightenment, I felt it would be a noble cause if one brought enlightenment to people. Spread the message as long as one could. And I decided to do it. I found out a plan for it. I wanted to do this, but with a difference. With a difference that this could indeed prove to be useful to people in day to day life rather than eating up their rest of their lives in dummy worship or saint-worship. I had a plan to do all this, but with a twist."

He paused.

"And what was that?" I asked as I saw Kaushal checking his watch as if this 'Prime-Minister' had a plane to catch!

"The difference was in the application," the Dean went on, "Unlike the other *Ashrams* where people went for relief, spirituality, enlightening self, giving up on their families and responsibilities to serve the *Gurus* and God, I wanted something simpler and more fulfilling. A place where people learnt about what life had to teach us with a touch of spirituality and go back to lead a peaceful and happy routine life without having to compromise on their family duties. After all, spirituality is not about running away from your *karma.*"

"So you're opposed to the age-old *Ashram* systems where people spent the rest of their lives to serve humanity and God?"

"No, I'm just opposed to the way people go on to abandoning their lives and families to seek God via these *Gurus* and *Babas*. You cannot run away from your responsibilities to be with God. During my stay in *Varanasi* I saw people from well educated families getting brainwashed, eventually abandoning their entire family to 'serve' the *Guru*. The teachings of the *Guru* in most of the *ashrams* were misunderstood. God never asked you to devote your entire life to serve some *guru* or himself by abandoning your family life and responsibilities. He just wanted us to be good people who help other people to cope with their problems. Very few good *ashrams* teach true life lessons; the ones that can be useful in every walk of life. I wanted to teach that. Not only in Varanasi, but everywhere I could. What is learnt there can also be learnt here in *A Way Around*; of course not like a PhD or a diploma, but whatever you learn here will be enough like a short spirituality-personality-development course in humanity rather than religion. Hence I came up with this *A Way Around* workshop which as you might know is of not more than 2 weeks in duration. People come; they learn and leave, being a better person probably. This is one of a kind workshop my friend, you'll see as we'll proceed."

"Sound's great Sir." I said.

"Yes, also as you know, we want to reach out to people, rather than their coming down hunting for us. So, we are always on the move! Every 6 months we change our locations, rather cities and towns to reach out to people and arrange our activities at some rented place like this one for about two weeks."

"For the last six years you also have been conducting these two week seminars at an international level. How was that experience?"

"Well we've conducted our workshops in select cities of countries like the U.K, Australia and Malaysia. We're welcomed everywhere and greeted with love. It's quite an experience and a great feeling you see."

The interview continued with a few more questions regarding the workshop and some other things in the same regard. Then I asked my last question which every reporter would ask to man like Rathod, "Sir, what is your message to today's youth?"

"Why only the youth, my message to anyone here is clear," Mr Rathod adjusted his glasses, "Do what you wish to do, without letting down anyone from your family. Enjoy life but learn to give too. Materialistic things are okay, but life is more about happiness and shared love. Also –."

Mr. Rathod couldn't even complete his sentence when

something weird happened. There was a ring. A cell phone ring! I quickly touched my jeans pockets as a reflex to see if I had by mistake forgotten to keep my 'digital distraction' back in my locker after checking it in the morning

"It's mine, don't worry." Mr. Rathod calmly reached his pocket and took out his cell phone, "Please see who it is and take care of it." he handed over the phone to Kaushal. Kaushal went out of the room to talk on the phone.

"Surprised ha?" Mr. Rathod was questioning me.

"Uh.. yeah well" I wasn't quite sure what to say.

"It's okay; we keep our digital distractions only to keep in touch with our disciples outside. Also, for you people it is banned here since this is a short 14 day workshop and you have to learn so much in so little time. You may live the rest of your lives with your gadgets, but here we need full attention of our students."

"Absolutely." I smiled.

"Is that it then? Anymore questions kid?" Mr. Rathod was generous.

"No sir, that's it." I thanked him and started dismantling my handy-cam from the tripod.

"So how's your documentary thing going? You have any troubles or doubts you can contact me directly. Just inform Kaushal in advance." Mr. Rathod said as he got up from his chair.

"Yes sir." I said.

Every institution has its own favorite teacher or professor that none of the students hate. In this workshop, Mr. Rathod was that one person.

✻ ✻ ✻

"So how did the interview go?" Karan asked me as he, Richa and I were strolling on the lawn in the workshop area post-lunch.

"Good," I said, "But a weird thing happened."

"And what was that?" it was Richa asking me, in a mocking

tone.

"That dude had a phone." I said blankly.

"Digital Distraction! Don't tell me!" Karan almost shrieked, "I want my iPod back now."

"Man, relax. Will ya?" Richa hit Karan playfully as we walked further up to the gate, "he'd better have an explanation for it."

"Yes he did, and I see nothing wrong in it." I said

Karan joined his hands in front of me, gesturing a sarcastic salute.

"No, I mean when you were in school, didn't the teachers ask you to not get digital fancy watches or use ball pens, while they themselves used or had those?" I explained.

"I don't get it. But anyways, they didn't sign the contract, we did. This is their place and their rules will apply." Richa said.

Karan didn't buy the explanation. It was a long shot. We continued walking.

There was a silence of about a couple of minutes, someone had to break it.

"We're allowed to explore the city whereabouts aren't we? We have two hours every day after lunch right for '*exploring the surroundings*' as the trainer said?" Karan said.

"Yes, we're allowed to go out." I answered.

"Provided that we do not carry our digital distractions with us, always wear this workshop t-shirt and carry no cash." Richa reminded.

"Then what's the point?" Karan sighed.

We had already kept our fancy gadgets and phones in our lockers first thing in the morning. At about 10p.m we were allowed to check into our lockers and have them for some personal use only in case of emergency. As all the food and eateries from breakfast to supper were arranged by the workshop itself, we weren't even allowed to carry our wallets with us. We could roam the city and explore the neighborhood in the 2 hours after the lunch, but without any of the above things and return by 4pm for the scheduled lectures.

Karan did not see any point in roaming around and exploring the neighborhood without cash, which also meant we had to walk as transport would require money, we decided to stroll inside the workshop property for today.

"We'll explore the interiors today; we still have many days of exploring to do! There's no point in going around the city if we don't shop or enjoy or even have a meal outside. I don't see any gain there, only pain." Karan said, "About turn!"

I chuckled, Richa nodded and Karan took a 180-degree turn from the gate as we walked back to where we started, circling the building and strolling on the workshop lawn.

'Then what's the use?', 'What will we get from this?', 'I don't see any point in doing so and so' were the timely arguments made by Karan whenever he wanted not to do a certain thing or procrastinate the same.

It's indeed true that everything that a person did, somewhere somehow was broken down into profits, gains and losses. Just like my decision of attending this workshop out of the blue to fulfill my hobby was being frowned upon as no one saw any 'profit' or 'use' in it. No matter how much you hate mathematics, these subconscious life-calculations of profits and losses at some level never leave you. Never.

CHAPTER FIVE

Day 3

"So tell me. Why do you think we have banned your digital distractions over here?"

'Wow,' I thought, 'What a way to start the lecture, a question to which almost everyone kind of knew the answer but still weren't quite sure.'

It was the third day and the second session of the morning.

Our usual yoga session was over, followed by breakfast, and now we were at the 'assembly hall' for our lecture *'How to live peacefully'*. It was quite an irony that Mr. Kaushal Prajapati was conducting the lecture, as by no means did he appear a peaceful or an inviting person by any angle, not to forget his stiffness and touch of arrogance in body language.

"Anyone?" Kaushal was scanning the class for some answers.

I scanned the hall. People were paying attention. Some were jotting down points in the notepads provided, which I found weird because the only sentence Kaushal had spoken till now was a question, which was yet to be answered. Then some were looking around just as I was, to see if anyone said anything.

Then I saw a hand, and so did Kaushal. It was Thomas.

"Maybe you feel it will disturb or distract your sessions?" he said.

"Umm… you see that is one of the reasons but not the one I'm looking for actually." Kaushal was quite happy it seemed that his question was not answered. Now he could come up with the real answer, the one which surprised the listeners or at least made him sound different.

There was a slight whispering after Kaushal declared that the obvious answer Thomas had just given wasn't the one he was looking for.

"You have to understand something here," Kaushal continued as he began walking to and fro on the stage with the mike in his left hand, "There's a strong reason that we call all your digital modern day equipments 'digital distractions'. Everything isn't necessarily what it appears on the surface. There's a greater purpose to every small thing that happens. Remember, a greater purpose. Firstly I would like to know how many of you agree on this with me. How many of you really do miss your fancy gadgets now that you've surrendered them to us for the next 13 days."

Not so surprisingly, almost about 80 percent of the hands went up. Karan was in the row just adjacent to me, with both his hands up! As if that would get him that iPod back which he had surrendered unwillingly. Richa had her hand up too, and so did Thomas and Stacy. Many such had followed the suit. I was so very engrossed in counting hands; I had almost forgotten to raise mine.

"Fair enough", Kaushal gave a little smile, which I found mechanical and pre-planned. This must be his routine thing for every such lecture.

Kaushal now started moving to and fro on the stage as he eyed his audience.

"Okay, you there. May I know your name please?" Kaushal said pointing towards the area where I sat. Initially I thought he had called out for me.

"You. Guy with both your hands up" Kaushal filtered his

search so that we knew exactly who he was referring to.

Now without a doubt, it was quite clear that he was pointing at Karan.

"You seem to be interesting. Both hands up?" Kaushal continued his to-and-fro motion. He definitely wanted some explanation for the over-enthusiasm shown by Karan in answering the question with both his hands up.

Karan now got up. I was looking forward to the upcoming conversation in the class now.

"So tell me, how badly are you missing your distraction?" Kaushal asked.

"More than we miss the tasty food outside." Karan answered.

'Whoa!' I had a lump in my throat, 'That was one nasty answer. This could get ugly now.'

Richa now looked at me from her place. She had that surprised look on her face too. It was like I was looking in the mirror.

"I see", Kaushal was calm, "And why is that?"

"I would like to answer that with a counter question, Sir", Karan was on a roll today, it seemed.

"Shoot, boy"

"How do you explain the fact that the 'digital distractions' as you call our devices aren't any distraction for some?" Karan said.

"I'm sorry but I did not exactly get what you're saying" Mr. Kaushal was confused, but I was afraid as I knew where Karan was heading.

"I mean," Karan continued in a calm tone, "Is the rule of distraction only for commoners or is the law same for everyone?"

"Of course the law is equal to one and all, no doubt. Also, just so you know, there's nothing such as a commoner or a non-commoner here!" Kaushal was confident on the answer, he then continued, "May he or she be a commoner or be any big shot builder or ministers' son or daughter, rules are rules and no one, believe me, no one is given any special treatment over here."

"No one? Really?" Karan asked in a stern tone now.

"No."

"So how do you justify the use of mobile phones for all your staff members? Isn't it a distraction for them?" Karan finally came to his point.

"See boy, first of all, this isn't any of your business," Kaushal pointed his finger towards Karan while he spoke now and I was afraid he would soon lose his temper, "But still I wouldn't leave your question unanswered."

Kaushal stopped his to-and-fro motion and continued, "Firstly it's you people who are here to gain knowledge and wisdom from us and will be here for like what, 14 days? So it's quite clear that for such a short term intensive course we would require you're entire attention. On the other hand, we are teachers. Just as in any school of learning, teachers are not banned all the things that students are banned of."

Personally, I was getting what Kaushal was explaining and thought Karan was fighting on petty issues without any reason.

"I don't agree Sir." Karan was in no mood to give up, "Just like you expect our full attention in your class, we too need your utter dedication while teaching us."

Now this statement of Karan was totally unfair because never had any one of the staff members had their phones ringing or other distractions while any class was on.

"I don't think this is worth debating now." Kaushal said as he moved his gaze away from Karan.

"So class, where were we?" Kaushal addressed everyone now, ignoring Karan.

The entire class was silent, still recovering from the out-of-no-where small spat that had happened between the student and the teacher.

Kaushal remained silent for about half a minute and then just decided to move on with the lecture.

"Anyways, so as I was saying.." he began.

"Can I have my iPod back?" it was Karan again.

"Boy, what is wrong with you? Seriously!" Kaushal was shocked.

I was surprised too; Karan now seemed to be deliberately pulling up a fight with Kaushal. I had no clue what Karan wanted to prove.

"Sir, this is just a question which you can answer with a yes or a no." Karan said.

"I will answer your question with a 'get-out'! Do not disturb the class!" Kaushal shot back.

Karan laughed, making Kaushal even more furious.

"Wasn't this lecture about *How to Live in Peace?* Why does my one question bother you so much Sir? Ever heard of practice what you preach?" Karan spoke.

Karan had crossed the limit now. I could see the veins on Kaushal's forehead popping out.

'This is it now' I thought. It was high time for me to get into this debate now for once. Not because I wanted to defend my friend but because there was something wrong going out there, and someone needed to stop wasting the precious lecture time in petty fights.

"May I interrupt, Sir?" I literally kind of shouted as I raised my hand.

"Wow, now you want to join too along with your friend?" Kaushal said.

"No sir," I kept my voice calm trying not to offend neither my teacher nor my friend as I continued, " Whether we agree or not on each others' issues or questions is a different thing, but I feel every single question and query here needs to be dealt with respect and so does every other opinion."

"Wow, boy" Kaushal said with a hint of arrogance and sarcasm in his voice, "Now you come here, and enlighten us with your views."

"We have been asked to come here with an open and neutral mind, ask questions and seek answers, and explore them." I continued, "But you, Sir, seemed quite uncomfortable with my friend's simple and silly question. I don't think there's anything wrong in it. But the way you reacted to this heated debate will prove only one thing.."

"And what is that son?" Kaushal interrupted, with more arrogance.

"The only signals you're sending here is that once you touch any sensitive organization related issue here in your questions and queries, you'll be denied of the respect as well as a decent answer or even a mere response to the question. This contradicts your basic principles of code of conduct in the workshop. Rule states that no one here is left unanswered and that too with such treatment, is unacceptable, Sir."

"This is enough now." Kaushal was upset now, "Either one of you leaves the class right now, or I stop the lecture."

There was buzzing again. Richa looked at me and shook her head in disgrace.

This wasn't how everyone expected this session to proceed. This Kaushal person surely had some problem. I always had an uncomfortable feeling when he was around.

"I will leave Sir." I volunteered without hesitation, "Rather than being treated like my friend on asking questions, I would like not to get an opportunity to ask any."

The moment I finished my sentence someone applauded loudly. It was Karan. He was looking very proud and happy seeing his friend standing up for him, but this wasn't the time to acknowledge it. I signaled to him to stop and sit down quietly, as I moved on.

Before I passed the door to move out of the class, Kaushal called me, "Boy, meet me today after the day ends. We need to talk."

I had seen this coming after all the drama.

"Yes of course." I sighed as I stepped out.

I saw Karan settle down in his seat, still upset. I just hoped he stayed quiet for the rest of the lecture now. I walked out of the class door.

I had about 45 minutes to spare till the next lecture after which we had our half an hour lunch break followed by the 2 hour 'exploring' time in the neighborhood outside the camp premises.

I walked down the empty hallway. Even though this was a huge *bungalow* it was built more like a small institution or a medium sized school, just like the old kinds that we see in the suburbs of the city. A person was watering the lawn and the small plants beside it. The sky was bright and the sun was high. Perfect. I thought.

"Hey boy!" someone tapped me from behind. The term 'boy' made me think that Mr. Kaushal had followed me to seek some kind of revenge for his hurt ego. But the voice was that of a female. It was Richa.

"How did you—." I was cut in mid of my question by her.

"Relax dude, and keep walking," she said as we walked further towards the back of the building.

"After you left, there was a discussion amongst the people inside the class," she explained, "And Kaushal then sternly asked if anyone was even interested in attending the remaining lecture or wanted to join you."

"Let me guess," it was already clear to me what could have happened, "you raised your hand or something?"

"Yes Sir" she said with a bright smile.

I laughed, "You are insane!"

This girl had walked out of the class after me for no reason again. I would've expected Karan to do it, but her doing it came as a total surprise to me. One bad side to this was that she too now did not have a nice impression on Kaushal. A good side to this was that I had company now.

We walked further as we came by the gate, the back gate to be precise which was like one of the emergency exits to the place, smaller than the front gate.

I was about to do a U-turn when Richa held my arm, "Let's go outside."

"We have our exploration time later; we'll go then." I said, "Anyways we have only about like half an hour before the next thing in the workshop."

"Oh c'mon." Richa was reluctant. She walked past the small gate onto the narrow lane street. I followed her.

"What are you up to?" I asked her persuading her to get back to the workshop.

"Nothing much, exploring. Letting my mind free." Richa wasn't making any sense to me now.

"Well this isn't the time!" I said

"Sorry, but I don't watch the time before I do whatever I like. If I feel like doing it, then it's the right time. Always." she said.

I was impressed. This is how people should be. People wait to start with their work until the auspicious occasion, but don't realize that the moment you start doing your thing without wasting time, is always the right time.

The principle didn't apply to our current situation in any way, but it was just a realization back then. I had found reasons to have a certain kind of inclination for Richa now and it wasn't just her beauty.

Her walk had now paced up a little. I had to brisk walk to keep the pace. Soon we came by a bus-stop at the junction of the lane that met another road.

Richa sat on one of the empty seats there. I was a little tired of the brisk walk too; I rested on the horizontal bar at the bus-top opposite her.

"So?" She said.

"So what?" I asked.

"Would you like some adventure?" She asked me. I'm not sure, but I guess she winked when she said that.

"Yes, I'm up for adventure any time!" I replied like a good sport.

"No, you're not getting me." She said, "Would you like some adventure? As in NOW?" She ended the sentence with a mild smile.

"Well.. uh.." I wasn't sure if it would be wise to accept a challenge without knowing what it was. But then, she got up abruptly from her seat.

"What happened?" I asked.

"Just come with me." she said as she held my hand firmly, "After all that creep Kaushal talk and lecture, we do deserve some adventure and day out for ourselves."

"What the—." I couldn't complete my sentence, yet again, as she dragged me literally out of the bus-stop. Then I realized something, a bus had arrived there. I gulped as my throat went dry, if only she's doing what I think she would do now, we'll be in trouble. A lot of it.

And without hesitation Richa climbed into the bus that halted at the stop. She held my hand, so I too without much realization and haste of things, climbed into the bus.

Only about 5 seconds into the bus, I heard the 'ting-ting' bell noise by the conductor and the bus moved on!

"What the hell do you think you are doing?" I screamed as we were trying to stand and make our balance in the moving bus, as it was moderately crowded.

"Everything happens for a reason." She said in a Kaushal like tone, "Remember, there's a greater purpose to everything. You may not see it now, but there is."

And then she giggled, again.

I wasn't quite sure what she meant by that, but this certainly wasn't called for. In my wildest of dreams, I never thought I would give up a semester to pursue a documentary mission, only to end up bunking a class with this new friend from Delhi, travelling in a bus to nowhere. If all this was a nightmare, all I wanted to do now was, wake up!

CHAPTER SIX

"Are you out of your mind?!" I was furious now, "You understand what you're doing don't you?" The bus had picked up speed and Richa had caught herself a window seat. I sat beside her; rather, she had dragged me beside her.

"Yes Sir!" she mockingly replied.

This was bizarre. In no time, this girl had gone from normal to insane.

"Okay listen," I said to her but she was busy giggling and looking out of the window ignoring what I had to say, "Listen Richa!"

Now she looked at me, "Shoot!"

"You understand what you're doing don't you?"

"Correction, what *we* are doing." she said giggling at me again.

'Great' I thought as I realized that it wasn't she alone that was going to bear the punishment, but me too, that too without any fault of mine.

"See, you might not have anything to do with this workshop thing and it's just the usual running out from home thing of yours, but let me make it clear to you. I have sacrificed my exams for this documentary thing okay!" I was almost yelling at her, she listened quietly and just motioned to me with her hand to bring down my voice.

"Vishy…" she began.

"Don't call me that!" I interrupted

"Why? Doesn't Karan call you by that same name?" she insisted.

"Now what are you? Karan? Anyways, this is not the time for that debate!" I was rather annoyed by her teasing and giggling.

"Calm down ya," she hushed me.

It shocked me how calm and composed she was even though I was getting so paranoid. Maybe because she didn't have anything to lose.

She then said, "See buddy, we are in this camp for like 14 days, out of which we are choosing to enjoy ourselves and get a little thrill out of this for like what, just a day. You're not losing anything on your documentary stuff. Don't get so much hyper-ish and all."

"Oh really?" I began again, "Guess what those people will say when we return afterwards? What will we answer? They're going to throw us out abruptly before 14 days."

"You are such a *dumbo*!" she giggled again.

"Vishy was way better than this new '*dumbo*' name thing now" I muttered. But then I continued, "I had a tough time convincing my parents, teachers or even friends that this was what I wanted to do, and now due to your stupid little adventure we will be thrown…"

"Slow down Mister!" she cut me half way, "I guarantee you nothing of that sort will happen. We're just out for a little fun. We'll be back for the 7.30pm '*Enrich Your Soul*' lecture. Also-."

"7.30!!" I exclaimed, "What are doing till 7.30! It's just 12 noon right now"

"Okay will you listen to me?" Richa said as she placed her hand on my shoulder.

I let her continue.

She adjusted her hair which was a little messed up because of the wind as she spoke, "I had actually planned this alone, sneaking out having some adventure and sneaking in back in the workshop without letting anyone ever know. I cannot take those lectures and life changing soul enlightening theories all day long. But then I thought now that you are my only friend in the workshop, it would be fun to include you in this too."

"And you decided on this without even asking me?"

"Of course you wouldn't agree if I had informed you earlier."

"This is not done." I removed her hand from my shoulder, "I'm getting down from this bus and heading for the camp, now."

"No wait" Richa stopped me again, this time placed her hand on my knees, kind of like pushing me back on my seat, "If you go now, firstly you have no money with you. Plus, people there will know that you weren't there for like an hour. If we wait till the 7.30pm lecture, it's been conducted by the new lecturer Mrs. Seth. She doesn't know who we are or that we are her students or whatever, so no questions asked there. Also, if you go by lunch time, we cannot have food because then we don't have the everyday lunch coupons which by now must already have been distributed. After lunch we have our usual 2 hours break where we can roam around the place so no questions asked there too because then everyone would be roaming here and there. Now comes the question of the after-tea session which continues up to like 7-7.15pm that is basically a nature trail around the place which is the only thing we will miss. Basically, everything and anyone missing by 7:30 will go unnoticed."

'Man!' I thought, 'This girl did have some plan.'

Before I analyzed her well constructed plan further on this 'adventure-ride' I thought of a greater problem, a temporary one for now.

"Speaking of money" I reminded her "Don't we have all our cell phones and wallets as well as other stuff in that locker back there at the camp?"

"Yes, so?" Richa still wasn't trying to understanding what I wanted to point out.

"So my dear friend," I spoke as I pointed her at the other end of the bus, "Forget all the adventure and what things we might have till 7.30pm, for now, how are you planning to pay that bus conductor?"

"I have my own ways." Richa said.

I was not sure what to make of that now, but just prayed it wasn't anything dramatic or filmy as it was happening right now.

"So *dumbo*", she continued, "You have two choices, either you get down from the bus at the next stop, go to the camp and do all the explaining about how you and me were missing from the camp for last hour or so, which obviously they won't believe because no one runs out just because someone they met 3 days before told them to. Or, you have the choice to have some fun and adventure apart from those boring lecture back there for today and enjoy the rest of the camp as we'll return back by the evening."

I didn't know if it was her convincing power or my stupidity, but she did sound reasonable to me now. I guess it was both. Now that I was a part of her plan, it was in my interest to play the part and enjoy myself rather than crib at whatever had happened. Plus how often do you get a day off to enjoy your silly adventure with a really beautiful and awesomely freakish girl?

I had a certain kind of liking for her by then; she did what she wanted, just like me. Without thinking of consequences, with head much more calm and composed than me and best of all she was a freak. I personally had a thing for independent people who didn't give a damn to what others might say or think and constantly think of the consequences. But there's a thin line between being brave and taking risks just to let your heart do whatever you want, and being mere stupid. I was afraid we had crossed it today.

I looked at her. Her beautiful brownish hair was blowing in to the wind from the bus-window. Her eyes were her most beautiful feature not forgetting the expressions those lovely pupils gave while speaking to you always making you believe that we didn't need to worry about anything but living in the moment.

I had calmed myself by now. That Kaushal guy had made my day already, in a bad way. I certainly deserved the company of this beautiful freaky friend. I was eager to know what plan she had in her mind for our 'adventure'.

"Okay Get down" she said.

"Sorry?" I wasn't sure what that meant.

"*Dumbo*! Get down from the back door of the bus at the very next stop!" Richa whispered.

"One more time you call me *dumbo* and I'm going back to the camp." I made myself clear.

She giggled again. We both knew that wasn't going to happen now.

"You never had a girlfriend, did you?" She asked hitting her elbow playfully at my arm.

"That is none of your business" I got up from the seat.

"Awww" she made a puppy-face as she continued, "That's why I call you *dumbo*. You are so very hyper and over sensitive guy. Also, *dumbo* is not a demeaning word you see! One day you're gonna like that word."

I ignored as her signature giggle continued from her side.

Then she got up and started pushing me through the crowded bus to its back door. The conductor would take like at least 3-4 minutes to traverse from the 2nd seat from the front to where we stood now. So we were quite safe that way.

"Get down, as soon as the bus stops." she ordered

"Can't believe I'm going to break the law. I've never travelled ticketless." I muttered.

"Dude." she gave me dead look, "It's not like we're robbing a bank."

That made me feel a little less guilty now. Just like I thought, this girl was different, could make you do anything.

The bus then slowed down. "Now!" Richa whispered from behind.

We inched forward. A few chaps hanging by the back door handle got down from the moving bus even before it halted. We made our way to the door finally.

And without hesitation and a ticket of course, we calmly got down as we started walking as if we owned the public transport system.

"See? Wasn't that easy?" She said as we walked further. The bus had moved on after dropping passengers at the stop, "You're such a *darrpok* I tell you"

"It's not about being afraid," I explained, "You don't need to break the law to display your bravery and get a sense of adventure."

"Yah yah." She was being sarcastic, "I too wouldn't have ever done this, but had no choice. It's not that we had money and still didn't pay."

I didn't argue further, for there was no point in it.

"So what next?" I asked her. I glanced at my watch. 1.10pm.

"I want the get rid of this workshop t-shirt first. We'll do some t-shirt shopping." She said.

"And how are we going to do that?" I asked, "Do not tell me you'll steal from the shop now!"

"*Dumbo*", she said, "We don't have cash. But ever heard of an ATM? We can always withdraw money from an ATM and use it. Though I like swiping card directly and paying for stuff, but then I usually avoid it. I usually like to take off cash from the machine and then spend it. Makes you aware of your balance you see."

"I'm not getting you, where will we get our cash from you said?" I asked.

"Ever heard of an ATM?"

"Great", I said sarcastically, "And you Ms. Richa, ever heard of an ATM card? As far as I know, the machine doesn't throw out cash seeing pretty faces. It needs a card."

"*Uff*" Richa shook her head in dismay, "Here you go."

She put her hand in her jeans back pocket and pulled out a visiting-card-like thing. No, it was an ATM-debit Card! This chick was damn prepared for everything. Literally.

"We could've paid for our bus tickets, you see." she said waving her ATM card, "but sadly, they don't accept these."

I had no idea what all this girl was up to. But she surely was one hell of a person to be with. I didn't know whether I was more surprised or shocked to see all that had happened yet. Little did I know that this was just the beginning.

CHAPTER SEVEN

About 45 minutes after our 'adventurous' run-away form the *A Way Around*, we were in a rickshaw, soon after Richa had somehow accessed the ATM centre to withdraw some cash. This way we could now have the luxury of not walking. Instead we could hire the rickshaw for travelling distances. Also, the cash with Richa made me thank God for the fact that our *rikshaw-wala* had his share of the luxury of getting paid by us, unlike the bus conductor.

"*Kaha jana hai madam?*", the driver enquired us after about five minutes of travelling, as the only instruction given by Richa 'madam' was to ride straight till she gave him any further direction.

"*Koi bhi najdeeki cinema hall le chalo bhaiyya,*" Richa answered.

Another shock for me. Richa had just ordered the rickshaw driver to take us to the nearest movie theater!

"We are going to watch a movie? Now?" I asked her.

"Yupp. Why?" she asked in a forced innocent tone, "You want to watch it tomorrow? I'm not sure if we could do this running away again tomorrow."

"I'm serious, Richa." I said, "What's wrong with you!"

This girl had gone completely nuts. I had absolutely no idea why she was doing this. The mere reason for this according to her was 'adventure' which didn't quite go well with me.

I really hoped she had a 'greater purpose' or rather a 'better purpose' at least if not a greater one.

"I think you're right." Richa said. I was relieved, until she continued, "We shouldn't go to the movies directly. We need to change our t-shirts first. I hate those workshop shirts they give. Plus we can't roam around and enjoy as per our will with this '*A Way Around*' printed on our backs and the miniature Dean-like picture on our chest!"

'Great', I thought, 'So now there's shopping involved too, along with the movie.'

It was hard fighting her. Even though all this bizarre turn of events were happening too fast for me to grasp, I saw no harm in just living in the moment and enjoying a day out with a new friend, who incidentally was a beautiful one and I think I had a mini-crush on by now. I had given up arguing with her.

I could see the *rickshaw-wala* enjoying our conversation and smiling to self. Great. Now we had an audience too.

After about a 20 minute ride in the *rickshaw* we reached a mall. It was a medium sized one as compared to the ones I had been in the metro cities. Richa paid the driver and then we moved further.

"So we change into new clothes and do what? Do you realize that we are going to need them again later when we return, so we cannot possibly get rid of them forever." I said.

"Yes, I know dear." Richa winked, or at least I thought she did, "We are going to get into our new clothes, keep these in the bag at the counter and then collect the bag while going the camp in the evening! Simple."

'Wow' I thought. This girl was sharp. She had a solution to almost anything under the sun. Moreover she made it sound so simple and straight! I nodded an 'okay' to her as we moved up to the entrance of the mall.

As we walked into the mall I realized how huge it was. It had about 4 levels connected with zigzag escalators and traditional stairways too, just like any other mall. There were the usual discount banners and people buzzing around inspecting things, filling their trolleys and baskets with the stuff they needed.

"They're all staring at us." Richa whispered.

"Why?"

"Weird flashy and same t-shirts?" she said, "First things first, we need to change them! Now!"

I nodded, if she said it, it had to be done.

Richa then went to a guy with the '*May I help You*' badge clipped on his t-shirt and asked him something, came back and informed me, "The casual clothing section is on Level 1, for both men and women."

She then literally held my hand and dragged me towards the escalator. The only person who had done this to me until now was my mom, that too when I was in school. I glanced at the digital clock that hung at the check-out counter. 2.35p.m, it displayed. About 6 hours from now we would be back in the camp, hopefully safe and sound and un-detected. 'Nice dream' I thought to myself. It wasn't so easy; I had no idea of what could happen when we get back there. Just like I had never known that all this would happen when I first saw and helped Richa.

✲ ✲ ✲

"Vishal how's this one?" Richa was out of the changing room again, for like the 6ᵗʰ time now. She was asking my opinion on her sleeveless milky green top. It went well the jeans that she had worn. Actually, I thought almost anything looked good on her.

"Nice." I said with a smile and an 'okay' sign with my fingers.

"What ya, you say this to everything I'm trying out!" she complained.

"I don't know but I like everything you're trying out!" I replied innocently to which she responded with a smile, or blush, or maybe both.

"Okay for the last time, tell me seriously, is this worth buying? I really love this one." she said adjusting her t-shirt and posing sideways in front of me.

"Can I use the F word to describe it?" I said playfully.

"Haan?", Richas' eyes widened with my reply. She didn't expect it, not from me for sure, "Well, yeah go ahead." she added with another wink.

"You look... FABULOUS", I said as we both burst into laughter instantly.

She shook her head came towards me and gave me a little kiss on the cheek.

"Such a *dumbo* you are I tell you!" she said as she walked back into the changing room. I watched her go, touched my cheek and smiled to myself.

Now it was time to buy me a t-shirt and get rid of the existing flashy one.

"We'll buy you a shirt instead of a t-shirt, it'll look good on you," Richa 'madam' had already decided what I should wear too! I was okay with the idea. Also, unlike Richas', my shirt-buying was done within merely 2 try-outs in the changing room and 10minutes, flat.

I had zeroed on a *Wrangler* casual half-sleeve shirt, with white and blue trendy-checkboxes on it.

"So how's it?" I asked her as I had the shirt on.

"Can I use the F word to describe it?" it was her time to play my joke on me.

"Yeah, please do." I said.

"That shirt is looking fucking awesome!" she said.

I gulped 'whoa she did really use it'. And the other couple

of people around us quickly turned to see who the one to be so excited was to drop the 'F' bomb in public. I held her arm and quickly hurried down to the level below to avoid further embarrassment.

"So now what?" I asked as we stepped on the escalator to get down to the level below.

"I wanna buy myself a bottle of nail-paint and maybe a lipstick" she said calmly.

"I'm assuming this is one of your jokes that I do not enjoy even a bit." I said

"No" she answered back as we stepped of the escalator now.

"God, now what? Buying cosmetics and stuff?" I had my hands on my head. When was this going to end!

"C'mon *dumbo!* I'm not coming to the movies like this! I need some glam-sham you see." Richa said narrowing her eyes as we walked further.

"Why do girls always need to look good 24X7?" I asked irritated.

"Because we want to get noticed! And boys like you won't even spare a look, if we look just like any other average chick." she answered.

"Is that some kind of indication to me?"

"Only if you think it is."

"Oh God, Richa, you are impossible." I shook my head in dismay.

"What are you? My dad?" she finally said a bit annoyed. I didn't answer.

We now walked to the cosmetics and handbags and stuff section on the ground-level of the mall. We had our new t-shirt and shirt on us, along with the price-tag on it. That felt quite weird. It felt as if we were one of those standing statues with clothes, only moving. In a carry bag that we had in our hands, we had placed the workshop t-shirts, which we would be later keeping at the 'check-in' counter with that watchman guy probably asking him to keep a watch on it till we came back and re-collected it before we went back to the workshop.

There were at least 60-80 shades of lipsticks and nail paints lined up on the rack. Richa hurried further to the display. I watched her. Her face lit up just like any school-going kids' face does when he sees the ice-cream van.

After about a couple of minutes of inspection she lifted two bottles of purple colored nail paint as she asked me, "This one or that one?" waving each of her hand one at a time.

"What's the difference? Both are purple." I was puzzled.

"What are you? Color blind?" She was shocked looking at my incapability to indentify the possible nano-difference in the shade of the paint bottle. Richa at that point of time made me feel with her look that it would have been okay if I did not know who the President of India was, but my failed attempt to differentiate the two shades of nail paint was an unforgivable crime.

"Okay the right one, that's better." I said though I was still firm in my mind that both were the same. Even if she applied one of the two paints to her left and the other one to her right, no one would even know the difference.

"Your right or my right?" She asked. Maybe she liked to irritate me.

I didn't answer, but she had got it. She kept one of the two purple bottles back on the rack and took the other one.

"Are you done now?" I finally asked her, "Or you want to buy a party wear or high heels to the movie?"

For a second I bit my tongue thinking that she might actually consider shopping for one of the two I had suggested, but to my relief she nodded a 'NO' and hit me playfully on my arm as we walked towards the billing counter.

While walking further I caught a glimpse of the new *Fastrack* sport watches lined up at a counter.

"Wanna see?" she asked me sensing my interest.

I nodded as we walked to that counter. I enquired about a

couple of watches that I had liked. Richa was ready with her suggestions like 'This will suit you. That one will suit you' etc. She was one hell of a shopaholic, the best I had met. She not only had interest and tremendous enthusiasm flowing out of her when it came to her shopping but while doing it for me too!

"This is just like the one Karan has, no?" Richa said pointing to a watch.

Then it struck me like a lightning. Karan! He must've gone bizarre by now! Looking, searching for both of us and eventually enquiring for us at the authorities! By no ways this was going to end the way Richa thought it would. Any other person at the camp would have never noticed that we or at least I went missing, but Karan must have instantly realized it long time back.

Richa had sensed by now that I wasn't paying attention to the watches at the display anymore.

"What?" she asked

"Karan!" I whispered.

She smiled, relaxed and calm as she placed her hand on my shoulder, "I know what you're thinking. Before I left the class after you, I told him that we might not be available for quite some time and do not spread the word. I told him I would explain later."

'Man. What was this girl?' I thought, 'Could she *ever* go wrong?'

I wondered if she said it just to calm me or had really notified Karan.

I was relieved for now. I did not know about Richa, but I surely had a lot of explaining to Karan after we got back. I focused my attention back to the watches displayed in front of me.

"So, you like it?" Richa asked as I tried out one of the brown-belt army style watch.

"Yes, maybe I'll buy this later." I answered as I placed the watch back on the glass table.

"Why later?"

"What do you mean by why later? I don't have money right now!" I said.

"Well hello!" Richa said waving her ATM card at me.

"No thanks." I obliged, "It's not like an emergency. I can come back later and buy it."

"*Dumbo.*" Richa began by addressing me as *dumbo* again, "I'm not gifting you the watch. You can pay me later!"

"That's not what I meant." I held her as I moved away from the counter.

"Oh my my!" she said dramatically, "So you're one of those!"

"What?"

"One of those, who don't accept money and stuff from girls! Ego gets in between, *haan*?" she concluded.

"That isn't the case either!" I was furious now, "If that were the case, I wouldn't have come in the *rickshaw* with you. Don't forget this shirt I'm wearing! You're paying for it right? Also-."

"Chill!" Richa almost shrieked, "I get it, chill." and then the usual giggling went on, the one that irritated me but the same that made me like her even more.

At the checkout counter Richa swapped her card as she did the payment for our shopping. We removed the price-tag off Richas' t-shirt and then my shirt. We placed our carry bag with the workshop t-shirt in it with the watchmen telling him that we would collect it after a couple of hours. He was reluctant to do so earlier, but the way Richa made a puppy face by pleading him to do it, he agreed. Not his fault. I would've hanged myself happily if a girl like Richa had pleaded like that.

We got off on the road now, looking for a *rickshaw* again, to take us to the movie theater. After about 5-7minutes later we got one.

"*Bhaiyya, koi Cinema Hall le chalo.*" Richa ordered the rickshaw driver.

"Oh wait" She said again as she turned towards me, "Aren't you hungry?"

"Uhh.."

"Anyways at least I am. We should have something to eat first, then the movie." She concluded even without letting me answer.

She then asked the driver to take us to a decent roadside restaurant. I just kept mum. She had to do what she wanted and there was nothing that I could do to stop her. I just hoped that we were done with this day as fast as we could.

We settled down now. Richa reached out to her jeans pocket and pulled out the bottle of nail-paint we had purchased. Just as I guessed, she had begun colorings her nails while we reached our next destination. I watched her colour her nails. Very carefully and with sheer concentration she painted each of her nails. Then suddenly she stopped and looked up at me.

"What?" she asked

"Nothing." I said.

She smiled, shook her head and continued with her job of nail painting.

CHAPTER EIGHT

"So tell me, how you feel now?" Richa asked me, while munching on her chicken lollipop.

"Sorry?" I was puzzled, by the question.

"I meant how you feel about our little adventure as of now? Shopping and stuff, lunch at a *dhaaba*. Enjoying yourself?" she asked, nibbling another piece of the chicken leg.

"First of all," I began, "This isn't a *dhaaba*. It just looks like one. I mean the appearance-"

"O ho!" she interrupted me instantly, "Too much of technicalities ruin the moment! You boys should learn a thing or two about '*being technical*' at the wrong place at the wrong time in front of the wrong people."

'Yeah Yeah' I thought, 'If she says it's a *dhaaba*, it is one. If I state the obvious, I'm too technical.'

We were now in a restaurant beside the little highway. We sat in the open area at the back of the restaurant with benches stretched out on which one couldn't sit and eat properly unless one sits with folded legs. This section of the restaurant had a Punjabi *dhaaba*-like look to it. Besides this and the fact that it served all kinds of Punjabi food, there was nothing like the authentic *dhaaba* feel in it. It was run by a South-Indian and the manager and the waiters buzzed here and there screaming and yelling orders to each other in a language I assumed was Tamil or Telgu. Neither were their *rotis* and *naans* as gigantic at as an authentic Punjabi-*dhaabas*, nor was the *lassi* thick enough. I wondered if any Punjabi-*jats* ran an *Idli-Sambar* chain in the north somewhere.

The *lassi* is one of my favorite cold-drinks, I hate it when it is messed with. Also, especially when it's the only thing I am having for lunch.

"So only *lassi*?" Richa asked pointing at my glass, "Aren't you hungry or anything?"

I looked down at her plate. The chicken leg lay on her plate, covered with red gravy.

"No, thanks." I said.

"Oh don't tell me you're a veggie!" she was alarmed as if I was the only vegetarian alive on the planet.

I nodded.

"*Dumbo*! Should've told me na!" she said as she dropped her spoon in the gravy quite abruptly, "We could have gone somewhere else!"

Only thing I was concerned about right now was that the chicken-gravy hopefully did not spill into my glass of *lassi* while she dropped her spoon which created quite a splash.

"No it's okay, anyways I wasn't much hungry and had a heavy breakfast at the workshop." I concluded.

She shook her head in dismay and continued with her *naan* and *sabji*, as I sipped on the *lassi*.

"Okay tell me" Richa broke the awkward silence after about a couple of minutes, "Any girlfriend-*shirlfriend*?"

I didn't know how do I was to respond to this one. I never had a girlfriend till date. Female friends, yes. But not that 'one' special person.

"No," I said, "Not yet."

Richa smiled again, kind of like making an expression that made me realize she already knew the answer.

With courage and some intuition that I would get a similar answer from her I shot the same question back at her, "And how about you?"

"I had." she said.

"Ohh!" that 'had' word made my heart cheer up.

"Three." she said again.

"What?" I wasn't sure if I got it right.

"I mean I had, three" she said.

I kind of choked on my *lassi*. Some of it came out through my nose.

Richa started laughing now. She offered me the tissue placed in front on our table.

"Dude. What world do you come from?" she asked, still giggling.

"A simple one." I answered.

Then we chatted, laughed and cracked jokes for another half an hour. Then it was time to go. I liked spending time with her. She was different, bold and independent. The perfect 21st century girl. I never had any girlfriend but she made me want to have one, just like her, if not her; only with a less number of boyfriends maybe.

✳ ✳ ✳

In the darkness of the cinema hall, Richa and I sat in the 3rd row from the back waiting for the movie to start. After about 10 minutes of debate or say a 'mini-fight' we had zeroed on to watch Danny Boyles' *127 Hours*.

It being a weekday and odd timing, the cinema hall wasn't filled to capacity. Only about 70 percent of the total seats were occupied and that too by boys and girls who might have flunked their lectures in the college and came out on their own little adventures.

"This one's based on a true story isn't it?" Richa whispered the question.

I nodded. The film was actually based on the true life story of Aron Ralston a mountaineer who got his hand trapped between the mountain wall and a boulder in the canyon while hitch-hiking. He had to eventually cut off his own hand to free himself from there in order to survive. A true story of sheer survival and bravery and filled with inspiration. Made you kind of understand that no problem was big enough that you could not get out of it.

The movie began after a couple of advertisements and a trailer of some upcoming movie. It was captivating. The scene where the protagonist slips into the canyon crack and traps his hand between the huge rock and the boulder, there was a collective 'Ohhh' from the audience. Richa held my arm tight for about half a minute. I felt nice. I guess I was the only person in the entire cinema hall having this feeling at the moment despite of watching what lay in front on the screen.

Then came the climax of the movie.

"I don't think I can watch this." Richa said as her grip on my arm had tightened. I joked about how I feared a blood-clot while she held my arm so tight and I might actually be following Arons' footsteps to save my arm. That joke was ignored. Not that I complained.

"Tell me," Richa asked, "Is he really going to cut off his arm now?"

"No dear," I said sarcastically, "He's just going to carefully un-screw the nuts and bolts in his arm to carefully dismantle it from his body and walk away free."

I was hit on my arm hard by Richa for cracking this one and this time it wasn't done playfully. I deserved to be punished.

"C'mon it's just a movie!" I exclaimed.

"Based on true story, right?" Richa eyed me.

Valid point. I had no answer.

The rest of the movie was watched by Richa acting weird and with narrowed eyes. She kept her one eye closed at times, as if it would make the gruesome amputation scene that was taking place in front of her in the movie more soothing. I was amused. This girl had the guts to run away occasionally from her home to make her parents agree to her demands, do adventurous stuff, and travel ticketless, but couldn't take a movie. I smiled to myself. Weird world, weirder people.

✻ ✻ ✻

It was about 6.30pm and already dark. Richa and I walked out on the not so crowded lanes towards the nearest rickshaw stand. According to Richa, we would be reaching the workshop by about 7.00pm and we would walk for about 20-25 minutes before we reached our destination. She said that it wasn't wise to stop the rickshaw right in front of the workshop, and we'd walk (or rather sneak) into the walls of the bungalow through the small exit at the back. Made sense; she always did, for some reason.

We hired a rickshaw and got off about 300-400 meters away from the workshop, as planned. Now we walked the remaining distance.

"So, now tell me. How was your day?" Richa asked me as we walked.

"Depends on how it goes from here." I replied, "The day isn't over yet! We have no idea what's waiting for us at the camp now."

"Uff !" Richa let out a sigh.

"On a serious note," I said as I stopped and looked at her, "The day was one of the craziest and most joyful one I had in a long time."

She smiled. Beauty. We hugged each other as a 'thank you' note. Then began walking again. After walking for about another couple of minutes with the awkward silence in the air Richa stopped again, and held my hand.

"You know, they say all guys are the same." She said, "But you are different."

"How?" I asked.

She stared in my eyes now. Silence. I saw into hers. Wow. These were the times when nothing else mattered. Neither the honking vehicle nor the buzz around us. I was awaiting my answer as I watched her looking into my eyes with her hands in mine.

"You're different because.... You're are *dumbo*! In a good way I mean!" she said as she burst into laughter.

'Bad joke' I thought, as I faked a smile too. This girl was now giggling uncontrollably.

"Awww look at your face, its red with anger!" She said as she tried to stop her annoying laughter.

"What did you think? I'm going to kiss you or something?" She still laughed pointing towards me continuing her 'funny' post-joke-laughter.

"No! I wasn't thinking anything!" I fought back, "Lets walk now!"

Then she did what I hadn't seen coming. Just like her, totally unpredictable.

She held my hand sideways, and with a small jump kissed me on my cheek.

I counted the score. It was two, in the last 12 hours.

"*Dumbo*!" she said.

Now my face was still red, but not with anger.

I quickly glanced around to see if anyone had caught the moment. To my relief no one was around in the vicinity.

"Awwwwwww look at you shy guy!" she teased.

Yes, I'm that kind of guy to whom a slap in public and the public display of affection brings in the same amount of embarrassment.

At some level, I thought Richa had started liking me too, at some I thought she was just that playful and friendly girl whose open friendly nature towards you could be taken in the wrong sense. But that wasn't my concern as of now. My only concern was the exit gate of *A Way Around* that was nearing us with every single step we took in probably our longest walk of the day.

CHAPTER NINE

"So here we are!" Richa said as we stood near the small exit-gate of the workshop. I faked a smile. I was petrified actually. We had no idea what was in store for us now.

Could they have figured out that we had sneaked out? Or did it go unnoticed due to the brilliantly scripted plan by Richa? If they had found out about our little adventure, what would be the consequences? Could they expel us? What if-

My thoughts were cut short by a screeching noise. Richa was trying to open the gate by pulling back the handle that was attached to a chain. It was locked.

"Shhhhh!!" I said.

I didn't want anyone to notice us sneaking in and we decided to climb up the gate into the workshop territory and make it directly into the class which would be filled by the students in the next five-ten minutes.

I helped Richa climb the gate first. The gate made some more noise, but fortunately there still wasn't anyone around. The two watchmen were busy guarding the main gate whereas the other two made rounds of the *bungalow* and had just passed the gate about a few minutes ago, so it would take them at least another 5 minutes to complete the round. With a thud Richa stepped on to the other side of the gate inside the compound of the workshop. I followed.

"Let's go now." Richa said, as she held my hand and we walked further towards the building trying to keep to the shadows. We somehow made it to the corridors of the building towards a hall to its end. People were already seated and there was the usual buzzing noise.

They were just back from the previous session.

The teacher for the current session was yet to come. Richa and I walked into the class casually. I scanned it, Karan was on the second last bench, and beside him was Mr. Khurana the retired army uncle. We hurriedly made our way to the last bench.

"I can explain.." I bent forward and whispered in Karans' ear.

"No need." He muttered. From his tone, it was quite obvious that he was furious. Richa had told him about us probably going out for a walk and not to make fuss about it, but he didn't expect it would last almost the entire day.

No complaints, he deserved to be angry.

Richa then touched my shoulder eyeing me, making an *everything-will-be-ok* gesture. For her it always was that way. Okay.

The lecture started after about 10 more minutes. I had no idea what all went in there for the next 1 hour. It wasn't my concern now. The feeling of being back from the adventure of Ms. Richa that too almost unnoticed, as of now, hadn't sunk in yet.

At about 8.30 pm the lecture got over and we were handed over the dinner coupons. We had dinner on the lawn. The usual Maharashtrian *thaali* along with some starters and sweet was served. I noticed everyone seemed pretty relaxed.

As Richa had rightly figured out, no one noticed our disappearance from the camp for about 6-7 hours. And the one who had, Karan, was silenced by her. He had chosen to have dinner with uncle Khurana and ignore us.

"We'll talk to him tomorrow morning, have your dinner now." Richa consoled me, "Right now, he's too angry even to listen to us."

I agreed.

This was truly unbelievable. An adventure, which could have and ideally should have ended with the expelling or at least strict action against us, had magically gone unnoticed!

Somehow, I wasn't feeling right. Or it was just the feeling of narrow escape that made me feel it. The sort of feeling you get when you know how narrowly you've escaped a mishap or an accident.

'Whatever happened had ended well. Without a fuss' I told myself, 'Tomorrow is a new day, and will continue as if nothing ever happened. Now just focus on your damn Documentary thing!'

"What happened?" Richa asked

"No, nothing." I replied

"Then eat no! *Dumbo!*" she giggled.

Her giggles made everything simple, or she herself made everything look simple and somehow tend to ease of such tense moments. Now that everything was settled, and I had my share of fun I reminded myself that I had a task at my hand from tomorrow.

I was happy. I was relieved. I thanked God for this. But still, that feeling of *'something-still-isn't-right'* was within me. We worry a lot at times it seems. And at some level we are so used to getting worried, that we worry why we aren't we worrying anymore when we don't have anything to worry about!

This was one of those times I assumed. Or was it?

CHAPTER TEN

Day 4
11.30 a.m.

I held my handy cam slightly above my chest level. Panning over the corridor of the place where our lecture-sessions were held, I then steadied it in front.

"Come this way." I was greeted by a welcoming Mr. Iyer. He had been the head of the food and nutrition department for the last five years in *A Way Around.* All the mouth watering *idli-sambar, upma, pohe* at the breakfasts, the tasty lunches and dinners that we all had, were due to this person and his team.

Today I had acquired permission to take a sneak peek at how the food and nutrition management was maintained at the camp and Mr. Iyer would be the guide for me through the tour.

I followed him through the hallway now as we spoke, "I've heard about you from my peers." he said, "You and your friend, created quite a buzz here the other day, didn't you?"

I wasn't sure if he meant Karan and my spat with Kaushal yesterday, or Richa and my escape adventure. I was very sure that it was the former, for, if it had been due to the escape adventure, we would surely have been detained by now. Also, even though I was happy that nothing had gone wrong as I had expected after our return to the camp after our day long adventure, I was equally amused by the fact that how was it that Karan had been the only person who noticed that we were missing for more than half of the day! Though we hadn't socialized much with other 'students' here for them to start missing us instantly within a couple of hours of our disappearance, but what about the teachers? Kaushal? Did he not notice too? Strange.

Or maybe the plain fact was that Richa's plan had worked as she had anticipated. Maybe no one noticed due to the given circumstances as explained by Richa.

"Are you listening, Son?" Iyer said.

My mind suddenly got back its focus on the task.

"Yes," I smiled as I followed him as he went on to explain stuff regarding his job.

"You see," he began as we walk through the door of the hall which led lead to a staircase, "More than a job, this is a service to humanity. I mean it's that feeling that you crave for and the satisfaction that you get from seeing the happiness and content you get on the people's faces. Feeding the hungry is the greatest service to humanity you see."

We now climbed the stairs and up there on the first level was the kitchen.

I knew it even before I could enter it. How? Obviously, because of the aroma of the food that was being cooked for the lunch. As we neared the kitchen on the left of the floor we could now see light fumes. I presumed it was of the *sambhar*. We walked further into the kitchen area.

About 8-10 men were working around in some sort of a semi-circle. In front of them lay big utensils in which they were cooking their food. There was rice, *dal*, and a couple of vegetables which I couldn't make out due to the not so thick gravy and fumes over it. The only recognizable thing I could see in there was the potato *sabji* as it had no gravy, not yet. These men were in the usual chef-like uniforms of '*A Way Around*' printed on it. Their hats had the workshop logo, which was an animated picture of a flame surrounded by a round-shaped arrow.

"It takes about 3-4 hours for these men and the women inside to prepare a wholesome and tasty meal for all of us," Iyer said, "Come in."

There was another room adjacent to this kitchen. Not as big as this one, but considerably large. That room had only women. Five women there were working on the stove and gas to prepare *rotis* and other additives like chutney, *papad* and other things that we would have along with our meal.

I panned my handy-cam to the entire room. The women looked up to see who had entered their territory, saw Iyer and me as he introduced me to them. They smiled and continued with their work.

"You win people more with their appetite than anything else." Iyer further said, "No hungry or un-satisfied stomach will allow the brain to concentrate on the stuff that you people are learning here."

He was right. I nodded. I was hungry already looking at the menu and losing my concentration.

Then I shot a few questions regarding how he conducted and managed his team and kept them organized during the workshop. He answered my questions in a satisfactory manner. I also learnt that the workshop had a 24X7 appointed doctor and nutritionists who planned the entire breakfast and meal schedules along with what all would be needed and stuff for the entire 14 day period.

I was impressed.

We talked for another 10 minutes or so, until we walked out of the kitchen to the first level corridor again.

"Walk this way." Iyer said. I followed. He now led me towards the door to another room diagonally opposite to the kitchen. This one was locked.

Mr. Iyer pulled out a key from his pocket to open it. After

playing with the lock for like half a minute he opened it. It was dark inside.

"This is our store room." Iyer said, as he went in and reached for the light switch. A dim bulb lit up the small room. It was dusty and bleak with two huge cupboards and some boxes that lay on the floor.

"I'll be right back." Iyer said, "Stay here."

I nodded as I motioned my handy-cam to the room. There wasn't much to see. Mr. Iyer had left the room now, why, I didn't know. I went near the boxes that were placed on one another. They were dusty too, like they hadn't been used for at least a couple of months. The cupboards had locks on sthem.

"Boy," someone called from behind.

My first assumption was that Mr. Iyer had returned. But it wasn't his voice. I turned around. It was Kaushal.

"Oh, Hi sir, Good morning." I greeted him.

"Yes, good morning it is! Isn't it?" he replied.

'Weird' I thought. I glanced at Kaushal. He stood there in a crisp ironed white shirt with khaki trouser. Also, he had a transparent plastic folder in his hand which had a few documents in it.

"I was here with Mr. Iyer, he'll be returning now." I clarified.

"Yeah , I know that." Kaushal replied calmly as he entered the room.

"Could you please switch off the handy-cam of yours?" he requested.

"Of course." I obliged as I turned it off and placed it on the pile of the sealed boxes.

"Now," Kaushal began as he turned around and shut the door behind him, "We need to talk."

I had a feeling now this wouldn't go on well.

"Talk about?" I questioned.

Kaushal walked towards me dramatically as he raised his arm to hand over the plastic folder to me.

"Boy," he began, "Now whatever I'm going to tell you, will probably be the most important thing you need to know out here."

"This is regarding what sir?" I was confused.

"Not regarding what," he said, "Ask, regarding whom."

I opened the folder as I saw it contained an admission form. On the right top of the corner was the photo of the person to whom the registration form belonged to. It was Richa's form. I instantly knew what this was all about.

"Sir, I can explain –." I was cut off by Kaushal by a 'stop' hand gesture made by him.

"You still haven't got it, boy," He said, "There's a lot more than what meets the eye. This isn't about what you think it is. We jump to conclusions so fast you see. You have the same problem. That is so not my purpose of meeting you like this. You still haven't seen the greater purpose why I am here, yet."

CHAPTER ELEVEN

You know how some songs have such a brilliant sound and it is nice listening to them in the beginning and then they tend to lose it all completely? Utter disappointment, isn't it? Same is with some people. Kaushal is one of such people. The moment he begins his talk he tends to get you mesmerized and then the opposite happens. He disappoints you.

"What greater purpose sir?" I asked him.

I still had the file in my hand. I had no idea why I was given that; neither did I know what to do with it.

"Now as you know we have a disciplined way of working over here. And we expect the same from our students too." he began.

I nodded.

"Do you really believe that you and that girl Richa could sneak out of the camp for like 6-8 hours or so completely without getting caught?" Kaushal gave a crooked smile as he took a step towards me, "Who do you think you were trying to fool anyways!"

"Sir, I said I can explain.." I said but he motioned me to stop with his hand raised with a 'stop' signal.

"This isn't really about you two sneaking out actually. We don't care." Kaushal was calm as he went on, "We did notice it within an hour of your sneaking out of the camp. We just didn't want you to know that we knew."

I was confused. Okay they noticed, but then after more than 12 hours of knowing it why was Kaushal confronting me with it? Why? I mean why only me? Why wasn't Richa called here too?

"All your questions will be answered boy." Kaushal said, as if he read my mind, "First tell me, how you know this Richa?"

"She's my childhood friend. Her dad and my father were –." I was cut short again.

"Tell me the real thing" Kaushal said, "Not what you told Ms. Puja. Not the lie that you told to the registration authorities the other day to cover her up."

'Whoa' I thought. They knew. Who I was trying to fool anyways as he rightly had said. Sooner or later they were going to find out, just not so soon, I thought.

"See, speak out the truth now. This could land you into more trouble than you possibly can imagine." Kaushal said glaring at me.

This was serious now. I felt the need to speak out the truth now. I told him sincerely how I had just helped a girl who needed help. She couldn't be expelled just for not having just a couple of signatures.

"I see." Kaushal unlike any other time, had patiently listened to me, "And what did she tell you?"

"What?" I asked.

"What did she tell you about herself. Who she is, where is she from. The reason why she is here!" Kaushal asked.

"I would not share her details with you sir!" I said, "Ask her if you want to know about her. Ask me about my details, I will gladly tell you. I'm not here to report other student's backgrounds to you sir."

Kaushal bit his lower lip with rage and instantly snatched the folder I had in my hand.

"You still don't get it do you!" he said as he pushed me with his free hand and I landed on the heap of boxes, "You either co-operate with us, or you're answerable to the police!"

'Police!' I thought, 'They're going to hand over us to the police for this?'

This was certainly worse than I had imagined.

"See, calm down. We need your help and so do you." Kaushal said, "Let me complete first."

I took a deep breath. I had a gut feeling that this was more than I was looking for.

"What this girl, Richa, told you about her history and stuff does not matter because almost about everything she told you, is false. Certainly not the truth."

"Why would she lie to me?" I was confused.

Kaushal ignored the question and went on.

"You know we run through our own background checks of the students once they're admitted over here, which is random. We may or may not even perform a check if we don't feel like. But for security reasons, we usually try and keep ourselves clear of any mishap or accident from any anti-social elements entering *A Way Around* as now we're not a local institute, it is acclaimed world-wide and spreading its roots all over. We have been receiving intelligence reports from the Government to be alert as our camp has been one of the many secrete terror targets or a 'safe-hideout' for goons or possible terrorists too. We have our own little private investigation teams. Almost 80% of the attendees are scanned and pre-checked for their background checks before even the workshop starts, rest procedure follows later along with the workshop." Kaushal explained.

"But why would any anti-social community look for your camp as 'safe-hideouts'? I mean they have to go through numerous checks over here and have so many restrictions on getting in even simple electronic devices like phones or mp3 players! What good can they do by getting into such a camp?" I was confused.

"Do you think that anybody can forge anything or do something bad only with an intension of spreading the panic or take lives of people or to spread terror by exploding bombs?" Kaushal asked me and continued without waiting for my answer, "This isn't the case. We as a workshop travel all over the world. We organize our workshops in quite a few of The European countries too now. Also, we aren't a Government body so we just check if the person does not have an illegal background or just that whether whatever information that person has provided is authentic or not. Our intelligence is nothing compared to the kind that the Government has. It's comparatively easier to infiltrate in here. And it's not about exploding or planting bombs, anti social elements can look into getting here just because we travel worldwide and so they can get access outside the country through us! The visa norms are strict if approached individually but kind of flexible if done via reputed organizations like ours."

"How?"

"It's pretty simple. The Governments trusts us. We have tie-ups and good relations with the visa authority of many of the countries and it is relatively easier to get a visa via us than appealing to them individually. Once a bad person is successful in infiltrating our camp and manages to make it someday outside the country, he/she will escape the very first moment we land there. It's complicated actually. I'd rather not get into the technicality and the legality of the stuff."

"Isn't it a too long shot?" I asked.

"It is actually, but we have been getting regular warning from the intelligence to be aware of any infiltration. We cannot ignore it. There might be attempts to get into our camp, we have been told by the Government. For what purpose, we aren't sure yet. But the reasons that I've told you are what we have to guard against. No matter how remote it might seem or how absurd it might look. We have to take care."

I nodded. I wondered what all this logic had to do with Richa.

"So.. As this friend of yours, Richa, was already a suspect in our eyes due to the missing signatures episode, we decided to take her case on priority and do backgrounds check on her depending on her form that she had filled. And guess what?" Kaushal stopped. He knew how to hold his audience.

"What?" I asked.

"It's fake. Every single detail mentioned in her form. Her address, home telephone number, and the college she attended. Fake." Kaushal paused to see my reaction.

I was surprised, or rather shocked to say the least.

"So she lied with the information on the documents, so what, now she's a terrorist you say or anti social? This is absurd Sir!" I said.

Kaushal smiled, looked at the ground and shook his head without saying a word.

"So she did fake her facts. But then what next? What does it have to do with me!" I asked seeking an answer.

"You've signed as her guardian haven't you?" Kaushal gave his not-so-famous crooked smile again.

I was given the taste of my own medicine.

"Also, boy, this isn't just a case of forgery. This goes deeper than that." Kaushal had more in store for me.

You know that feeling when you are full after having a wholesome meal and your dear relatives force you to have just one more bowl of sweet? I had the same feeling right now, and wasn't even being overfed with sweet. This time it was information.

"So when we did find that she had faked all her facts on the form, as a part of our further investigation, it was our duty to get in touch of with her 'real' guardians and let them know about her. Then it would be our duty to hand her over to her real guardians, thus teaching her a lesson. We thought this was just another case of a 'adventurous' young kid who was out from some crazy 'outing' of hers."

I was listening.

"Then, all we needed was to confront her the day you both escaped. We searched every possible corner here, but in vain. Then we questioned your friend, Karan, who too pretended that he too was searching for you."

"Believe me Sir" I was apologetic, "I on behalf on both of us, I'm extremely sorry for the trouble Sir. I promise-." He cut me off again, with the sign of his hand.

"Did I say I have finished yet?" He stared at me.

"Sorry Sir." I said.

"Now whatever I told you till now, was just the tip of the ice-berg." Kaushal went on, "As I told you, the two you had suddenly got away, we didn't know for how long, so we raided your lockers for some stuff.."

It didn't surprise me even a bit. We deserved this.

"And guess what we found?" Kaushal shot a question.

I gave a puzzled look.

Kaushal nodded his head in dismay as he put his hand into the pocket his trousers and reached out to something. In his fist he had a small plastic device of the size of an eraser or smaller than it to be precise.

'What the hell is that now?' I was thinking.

"We found this in Richas' locker. Yes, this is our worst nightmare boy." Kaushal spoke again, looking at my expressions, "This is nothing, but some kind of state-of-the-art advanced transmitter device, audio or just location transmitter I'm not sure of that yet. Even the police have to apply and approve in advance with the Government if they need to use anything so high-techno. What was it doing in your girls' locker? She isn't a cop for sure, which leaves us to one hell of a scary conclusion... "

I gulped. I wasn't sure what to say now. How? Why? Who? All of these questions had made an army of their own and attacked me in full force.

"Oh boy!", Kaushal said as he pressed his hand on my

shoulder as he mildly squeezed it, "I'm afraid; you have a lot of explaining to do now. A hell of a lot."

I stared at the device that was being held by Kaushal. I had only seen such things or heard of then in the movies or TV Serials. I wondered what that transmitter thing was doing in the girl's locker with whom I had one the best adventures till date.

'Seriously Richa, who are you?' I wondered.

CHAPTER TWELEVE

Earlier that day...
Hours before the talk with Kaushal in the store room..
7.00am

"Seriously, what are you looking for?" I asked Richa. We were at our lockers checking our cell phones for any calls or sms as we did every morning and late night, just in case to check if there's anything important was to be addressed to the outside world.

We were allowed to do this twice a day; once in the morning, and once before going to sleep at night. Richa had checked her phone but something was still bugging her. She was looking for something in her locker. Something she hadn't found yet.

"May I help? What is it that you're searching for?" I offered my help.

"Naah, you need not know. Please let me search." She said busy going through the locker. It seemed urgent. It wasn't something casual that she had missed. It seemed urgent.

I just stared at her from behind peeking into her locker to see if I could see anything or be of any help to her. Then she realized I was looking, and turned back slamming her locker shut instantly.

"It's nothing you see, just looking for one of my ear rings, my favorite ones and can't even remember where I kept them." she tried to convince me.

But it wasn't her earrings for sure. I had never seen her wear any in the last four days. But it was none of my business.

"So did you speak to Karan yet?" She asked me abruptly changing the topic.

"No, he had already left when I got up." I said.

"Don't worry we will talk to him. I will talk to him." Richa said trying to console me. I smiled at her.

It was time for our Yoga class as per schedule and we decided to talk to Karan soon after it, during the breakfast.

Now as we walked from the lockers towards the lawn area where our Yoga session would be held as every day, I spotted Karan there. He was busy warming up in a corner before the session.

Soon the Yoga session began, with the regular *pranaayam* and other simple *aasans*. My mind wasn't in the session. All that mattered to me right now was how to explain to Karan about the situation we had put him through. We owed him an explanation; I owed him an explanation.

"Students," the instructor addressed us after the session was over, "Before you disperse to the breakfast thing, there's an important announcement."

Everyone got up from the lawn standing, listening keenly to what he had to say.

"We are now distributing specialized ID-cards for each of you. Make sure you have them till the time you are in the camp and outside till this workshop is over."

There was a buzz. It was quite odd that these workshop authorities had suddenly decided to distribute ID-cards to the students after four days of the workshop. According to the instructor, this was the first time such an activity was being carried out. I somehow had a hunch that this had certainly something to do with our adventurous venture yesterday, but my mind back then was unable to process this fact as to what difference would it make to us by giving out these cards to all the students.

"Is that clear?" the Yoga instructor said loudly. It was the maximum decibels he had reached in the entire four days of Yoga session.

"Yes Sir!" a chorus of answers to the question was thrown back at him by all the students.

Soon, we had made a queue to collect our respective ID cards from the office. Each one of us wore it around our necks as we then walked again towards the lawn area, where our breakfast would be served.

I thought this was the correct time to talk to Karan now. As we all made our way to the lawn towards the tables where the breakfast was lined up, Richa and I hurried to catch up with Karan who walked ahead of us.

"Hey, please listen." I said, as I walked beside him as Richa followed.

"I don't want to!" Karan now walked faster as we tried to match his pace.

This was it. Now I had lost my patience. I held his arm tightly and made him stop.

"What's wrong with you?" I kind of shouted.

"Calm down you two," Richa came to us as she parted me and Karan making sure that we don't create a scene, "Tell us Karan, what's that bugging you so much? Did I not tell you that we would be away for while yesterday?"

"For a while, as in what? The entire freaking day!?" Karan was furious now, he then continued softening his tone, "You know, these workshop authorities were looking for you two! They had come to me to ask about your whereabouts!"

'Whoa' I thought. This was a shocker for me. Very conveniently Richa and me had sneaked in yesterday and slept well the entire night thinking that we had escaped a possible calamity. But this wasn't the case.

They knew! They had even confronted it with Karan.

'But why wasn't any action taken since they had already found out about it?' I thought as I looked at Richa. She had the same puzzled look as I had.

Why did the authorities not confront us with questions and try and hunt down the truth about where we actually were the entire day even after they knew that we were missing?

"And what did you tell them?" Richa asked Karan.

"I said I have no clue, you two suddenly disappeared and I too am looking for both of you." Karan told us.

Good. I thought.

But still, the authorities' maintaining the secrecy about not letting us know that they knew, was troubling me. It was only through Karan that Richa and I knew that the authorities knew about our little mis-adventure.

This was probably the first time I understood the meaning of 'deafening silence'.

This silence on the part of the authorities was something we weren't prepared for. It's funny actually when you're all prepared for the worst but then when it doesn't hit you, you become vulnerable!

We then started walking towards the lawn.

"Don't worry. We'll handle the situation when and as it comes. If at all it comes." Richa said in her usual take-no-tension kind tone.

"I'm sorry." I said to Karan as I placed my hand on his shoulder.

"Hmm." Karan accepted the apology somewhat reluctantly and added, "And don't you both dare to do such stuff again"

Richa and I nodded.

"And if you do, next time just do not forget to include me too!" Karan finished his sentence as we all burst into laughter.

All of us had our breakfast cracking jokes, discussing the workshop lectures and other such things. After that we had about an hour of 'Health Counseling' lecture in Class-4 which was a room adjacent to the workshop office.

"Vishal, can you come with me for a moment?" Richa whispered into my ear as Karan left us to get more of the *chutney* from the breakfast table.

"Yeah sure," I said as I got up and signaled to Karan 'we'll be back in a moment' who was at the table serving himself.

I walked behind Richa as she made her way through the lawn towards our lockers.

"You know we are not supposed to open the lockers now –."

"Shhh!" Richa stopped me by pressing her finger on to my lips, "Stay quiet!"

She took out a key from her pocket and opened her locker. I wondered what this was all about, but preferred to stay quiet as she had instructed me to do so. In between I glanced to my left and right to see if anyone in the hallway was watching us.

Richa finally took out an object from her locker and gave it to me.

"Here take this." She said.

"What is this?" I asked as I examined the object in my hand.

It was a metallic box about the size of a match box, or a little bigger to be precise. It had five dials which contained alphabets. Just like one of those bicycles' combination locks. The only difference was that a bicycle combination lock consists of three dials with numbers 0-9. This had five dials with alphabets from A to Z, obviously making the guess-work next to impossible to crack open it. So this was a secret box which could be opened only by setting the correct combination of all five alphabets. But why was Richa giving it to me?

"Ever read the *Da Vinci Code*?" She asked.

"Yes, that's one of my favorite Dan Brown books!" I said.

"This secret box is somewhat similar to the one in the book. I got this one from China last year from a random exhibition gallery, where I had got an opportunity to go as an exchange student. All you have to do is set a combination as a password and place the secrete message into the box and lock it. Now, only when you have the proper combination, will the box open and you can acquire the secret message written on paper in the box. If you try and break it open there's a chemical placed inside in a thin layer of coated glass that breaks, and with it destroying the secret message."

This was just like that secret roll in the *Da Vinci Code*. The scroll that was placed inside the cylinder (in the book by Dan Brown) was made of papyrus roll and would dissolve in the acid if the container that contained it was damaged or forcefully opened without the right combination.

Richa opened the box by taking it from me and pulled out a roll of paper from inside it. She then reached for a pen that she had taken from her locker along with the box and scribbled something on the paper. I had no clue what all was going on. It felt as if I was in some Bond film or in dream or maybe both. Richa then placed the tiny roll of paper inside the box as she closed the lid and started setting the combination lock. I watched as she did so.

"Oye! Look away!" she said.

"What I'm not supposed to look while you set the combination? How will I open it then?" I asked

"I'll explain, just look away from here while I set a password."

I turned my back towards her as she set her password for the combination lock.

"Look now." She said and I turned back to her.

She handed me the box as she spoke, "See, this is no joke. Looking at the bizarre events I have a feeling that you or I might get into deep trouble soon. All I want you to do is follow whatever is written in the message inside this box and you'll get all your answers."

"But how will I even open it!"

"See, I'm not even sure if you'll ever feel the need to open it. Rather consider yourself lucky if you never fall into such situation! Just know one thing I'll let you know the password somehow and you will get it all."

"But why not just straight away tell me! Why this 'secret box' drama!?" I quizzed.

"Because I'm not sure if you need to know the information in it yet. But in emergency you will, hence let it be with you, but only accessible when necessary." Richa answered

"Richa, I have no idea what you're talking about"

"Uff *dumbo*! I know this is weird. You don't have to know anything right now. It's just a possibility. This is very much important to me and will be for you in times to come. I cannot explain and make you understand all this right now, but I may not be into position of making you understand or hand over this to you later. Hence I'm giving it to you now."

"But then how do I know when to open it?" I asked

"You'll know. Trust me. Also, promise me that this will be the last option if you ever decide to open it."

"Yes."

"Also, do not discuss this with anyone, not even Karan. Do not share this box with anyone. This is purely between you and me. It all begins when this box is closed, it all will end once this is opened. So open it only when you think it's the end." She concluded.

"End of what?" I asked to which she did not even bother to answer.

I had made up my mind now. This girl was officially mad. No doubt. I took the box from her and placed it in my locker.

"And yes, now don't ever discuss this topic with me in front of anyone or even when we are alone unless I tell you to. Okay?" She asked

"Of course, anything else *memsahib*?" I asked mockingly.

Richa smiled as she hit me on my arm playfully and muttered, 'Idiot'.

We both giggled this time as we walked back towards Karan who by now had finished his breakfast.

"So private talks and all *haan*?" Karan winked at us the two of us approached him.

"Yeah, we're getting engaged." Richa said as my heart skipped a beat.

"What!?" Karan coughed, literally.

"I was joking stupid!" Richa said, as I realized that it was okay to breathe now. This girl could give·you an attack. And that's what I liked about her. The flamboyance and un-predictive nature in her.

"So what next?" Karan asked me.

It was the lecture on 'health counseling' waiting for us as later soon after that I had to take my documentary mission further. I had my appointment fixed with Mr. Iyer, the head of the Food and Nutrition department at the camp at about 11.30a.m.

'Today I'll get some more interesting photos and videos for my documentary' I thought, as we walked to the Class-4 for the lecture. Little did I know that that a mere interview and shooting session with Mr. Iyer, the head of food and nutrition department here was just the beginning and later I would be confronted by the person I hated the most in the camp, Mr. Kaushal, about the girl who I loved the most here, Richa.

CHAPTER THIRTEEN

Present time,
In the store room with Kaushal

"So boy, tell me. Are you with us or against us?" Kaushal threw his question at me. I felt a little threatened now. We still were in the dimly lit room. I stood there motionless taking one blow of the shock at a time, as given by Kaushal.

"Sir, I have no idea. With all due respect to you sir, how do I believe you? And if this is a case of snooping in your workshop with transmitters and stuff then why aren't you speaking with the police right now rather than me?" I put my brave foot forward. I needed some concrete answers and logical reasoning before I believed even a word that came out of Kaushal's mouth.

"Boy, you see, we have a reputation to maintain. Police and Government investigation will invite the media. And that is the last thing we want here. This, if not handled properly will blow out of proportion, which might lead our institution into trouble."

"And how is that? You aren't at fault are you?" I asked

"Yes, but the media. They always target the bigger fish to gain their TRPs. Stories about our institution being a 'safe haven for terrorists and anti-social elements' etc. will be run in their prime-time slots. They in turn will carry out their own 'Expose' coverage with hidden cameras and media agents. It's all about reputation my boy, reputation. It's very easy to lose it all, very difficult to get it back. We will be projected as the unsafe international-level organization and other countries might consider restraining us from granting permissions to conduct our workshops because this. Now that we're international, it isn't so easy."

"So you'll never let this out then?"

"Of course we will. But only when we for ourselves are sure what the situation is really about. We first want to conduct our own investigation up to the core and then hand it over to the Government investigation agencies with our findings and proofs."

"What difference does it make? Sooner or later, the Government and media will be involved. Right?"

"Yes. It does make a difference. When we hand over the case to the Government with our thorough investigation and strong evidences the media will cover it accordingly, restoring the faith in our own private investigative agencies and intelligence. We will be projected as an internally strong organization capable of tracking any mishap or anti-social units that try and trespass our security, which we are."

"I get it," I admitted, "But why are you telling me this?"

"This is the point where we need an insider to help us with our job."

"A what?"

"Insider. You and that girl Richa get along pretty nice since the first day. We want to make use of your friendship to access other information or bug-devices or ill fated plans that she might have."

"I don't think I can do that." I shot back.

"Listen, do not get emotional and all" Kaushal had expected my resistance it seemed, "Now when you do not co-operate with us, you are indirectly supporting the evil, the wrong, a possible culprit. The only reason we are asking for your help is because of your strong bonding with her in such a short time span. Also, fortunately for us, you are this documentary maker over here with your gadgets and stuff and have special permissions to film and record certain areas over here. You are on a mission known to everyone, so no one will suspect you of snooping into other stuff as they'll think that you are doing one of those filming things of yours. You could be collecting hard evidences even without anyone knowing you're doing so."

I listened as he continued.

"If you promise to help us, we will provide access to whatever you want in this workshop to make your documentary the best. No rules, no editing rights will be with us. You ask for it, and we'll present it to you, my word. All that matters for us is our workshop is safe, and its reputation is not hampered."

"But what if all of the things you are assuming about Richa aren't what you think they are? Maybe it isn't such complicated as it looks? She may be innocent!" I said.

"We would be more than happy if that were the case." Kaushal smiled, "But no ordinary girl carries transmitters and high-end snoop-devices and stuff along with her in a workshop where even cell-phones are restricted, you get my point? Also, we want to know the truth that's it. If in your findings you find that she is innocent then nothing like it. It's not that we are after her; we just want to find the truth. And if she is up to anything wrong, we demand justice."

Kaushal was finally making sense. Clearly, Richa wasn't confronted because they did not want to alert her.

"Okay I'm in." I hesitated, "But I would like to make one thing clear. I am in this only with a neutral mind. If I find her guilty, it's up to you to decide the action, but if not then I want us to be left alone without making any fuss."

"Yes of course!" Kaushal said.

Suddenly, the thought of the secret box crossed my mind that Richa had handed over to me earlier in the morning. I decided not to speak of it until I was sure about it. Also, I myself did not have a clue about the secret that it held and the password using which it was locked and no one would believe me if I even admitted that I did not know the password to the gift I had received!

It was too much data to grasp.

"So when do I start and what do I do?" I asked Kaushal

"As early as possible. Say, from now only. The first thing you got to do is get some or any of her digital distraction to us for a couple of hours"

"Like what?"

"Her cell phone, for instance."

"That's not possible! She'll know." I gasped

"No she won't. See you check your lockers every morning and before you go to sleep. In between there's hardly anyone who accesses lockers. I mean you are not even supposed to. So if you get us her cell-phone I'm sure we would get a lot of information."

"You had raided our lockers while we were out of the camp as you said. That makes it clear that you obviously have the duplicate keys to our lockers and you can frisk them whenever you want." I said, "So why do I have to do it? You can go on with your plans whenever you like!"

"There's a lot of risk involved. We don't even know if she's alone in this or any other person from this camp is also involved in it. You are like neutral third party agent to us. She would never suspect you and I guess you doing it will be safer as a student snooping around the lockers is okay, but authorities fidgeting with students' locker would be frowned upon. Also from the time when you hand over her phone to us, to the time you put it back again, you can keep her occupied so as to not make her want to check the locker."

"It's too much of a risk sir."

"Life is a risk boy. Right now, you have no choice. Think this as your service to mankind. Service to us. Do the right thing."

Kaushal made sense finally. I had nothing to lose. If Richa

did not have anything to hide then she had nothing to fear even if I did some investigation and handed over her phone to the authorities for a while. If she was guilty of something that posed a potential danger to anyone or the workshop as they claimed then her real identity should be revealed.

It was difficult for me to digest the fact that Richa could harm to anyone. She could be a little weird, adventurous and crazy but she would never be the one who Kaushal described as anti-social or terror-element.

I now wanted to do this. Help Kaushal in seeking the truth. I wanted to gather all the evidence that proved that Richa wasn't the one that they were assuming her to be. More than that, I wanted this to be done for myself.

'She is innocent, and will come clean' I said to myself.

Sometimes you just console yourself with your desired result even before trying out the test. This was one of those times for me.

CHAPTER FOURTEEN

After the weird and uneasy confrontation with Kaushal, I pinched myself a number of times after the incident, only in the hope that I would wake up from a nightmare. Now getting caught for the escape a day before and being expelled from the camp seemed a very soothing and desired outcome as compared to the current turn of events. This was like one of those things where another longer line is drawn in front of a line which makes it look shorter without erasing it. I was worried about getting expelled, but now getting involved in a possible high-drama-expose was even more worrisome.

As I approached the lawn, Richa and Karan came towards me. I watched Richa, she raised her eyebrows in curiosity as she spoke, "So? How did it go?"

"Uh.. well, okay." I said.

"You got what you wanted? How's that Iyer guy? And what's for lunch buddy? I'm sure you've got a good preview into the kitchen today." Karan patted me.

"Ah, well I did get what I wanted, rather a lot more than I thought I would," I said as I looked at Richa.

'Those pretty eyes couldn't do anything wrong' I consoled myself yet again.

But then I couldn't make the eye-contact stay for any longer. It was weird.

"Okay, let's proceed to the next lecture. Isn't it about to start in like 15 minutes?" I asked.

Both my friends nodded as we walked further.

CHAPTER FIFTEEN

Day 6

"What is the matter with you Vishy, you've been acting weird since yesterday." Richa questioned me as we walked through the lawn after the lunch break.

"You think so? No, nothing." I replied casually. But, no matter how much I tried to pretend normal, the doubt that Kaushal had put into my mind about Richa was disturbing me. I somehow wanted to do as Kaushal had told me quickly, and clear my mind. I hoped she had nothing serious to hide as suspected by the workshop authorities.

"I think that too!" Karan chipped in, "You've been quiet since the day before yesterday. Everything alright?"

"Yes, I'm just a bit nervous about my documentary thing." I lied.

"Aaah, don't worry *dumbo*! I know you will rock!" Richa said.

"When will you stop calling me *dumbo*?"

"When will you understand that I can't? I thought you're used to it by now." Richa giggled, "You'll like it someday."

There was no point arguing. We walked for about 20 minutes

more when Richa spoke, "Could you guys excuse me for a moment? I guess I forgot my ID card at the lunch table."

Her ID card was missing. She had removed it while having lunch because it hung on her neck till way down on the table tasting her curry in the dish.

This was just what I wanted, a moment with Karan.

"Hey, listen to me carefully now Karan." I said as Richa had walked away from us to get back her ID card.

"Shoot."

"Now what I'm going to say to you is very important." I lowered my voice so that no one else would even accidently hear what I had to say.

Karan was in attention now, as I spoke further, "I need your help. I need you to distract Richa for about 15-20 minutes."

"What for?"

"Don't ask. Just trust me. I want you to distract her and make sure she stays here with you here for about next 15mins or so and do not allow her anywhere near the locker area."

"What?"

"Will you or will you not?" I needed a confident answer here.

"Of course I will." Karan was puzzled, "But I need a strong reason for doing so. I will distract her here and what are you going to do at the lockers?"

"See, I will explain this to you once everything is settled, but right now I want you to do just what I am telling you to do. Trust me; I will explain everything to you once we're done with this."

"Done with what?"

"I need something from Richas' locker."

"Then you should've just asked her. She won't say no to you."

"No, she doesn't have to know. This is quite complicated."

"But then how will you access her locker without the key?"

"I have it." I said as I displayed a key from my pocket.

"You stole her key?!"

"No, the authorities gave me. It's a master key." I answered

"Don't tell me that the authorities are involved in this too! What are you up to man!" Karan was getting too many unpleasant surprises at once.

"Karan, this is important for us. For me. So I would be happy if you do not ask any more questions and –."

I was cut in the middle as I saw Richa nearing us.

"That was fast!" I smiled at Richa as she came back with her ID-card.

"Yeah, that Thomas guy had seen the ID-card left on the table and was coming here to hand it back to me. Met him even before I reached the lunch area."

We then again circled the lawn for about 5-10 minutes when Karan suddenly touched his knees on the ground covering his face with his hands.

"What happened?" I asked as I too bent down to see what was wrong.

"I'm feeling dizzy, my head is spinning. All I can see is black spots in front of my eyes." Karan spoke in a feeble voice.

"Wait I'll get water." Richa said as she prepared to leave urgently.

Instantly Karan held her hand as he spoke, "No, you stay. Vishal, you go and send in the workshop doctor too!"

"Okay sure" I said as Richa stopped and sat near Karan.

"Vishal" Karan said as Richa sat beside him, "Please make it quick."

And now I understood that this was Karans' plan to keep Richa occupied and give me some time to do the task I had at hand.

I ran across the lawn inside the building. Soon I saw the onlooker students had realized something was wrong in the lawn and they too rushed towards Karan, making a circle around Richa and him.

Someone called for help for Karan. Everyone was rushing towards the lawn thinking of it as an emergency situation. This was just what I wanted. At least for the next 10 minutes almost all the staff and curious students would be at the lawn scene whereas I could do what I was told to.

I hurried to the lockers. I was nervous and my palms had started to sweat. I glanced left and right. No one in sight. I quickly placed my hand on Richa's locker as I took a deep breath.

'This is it' I said to myself as I fiddled with the key and managed to open the door to the locker.

I scanned for any electronic device inside it. There were a couple of keys inside, a purse, some clothing, a ladies wallet and a cell-phone.

I grabbed the phone and watched it for about 10 seconds turning it in all directions.

It seemed a simple normal phone of a popular brand Nokia, without even a camera installed in it. That made me feel somewhat relieved.

'She cannot be a spy or a terrorist' I told myself, 'I just have to prove that to the authorities'

But there was no denying the fact that Kaushal had found a transmitter in her locker.

But then that's what he said! We're not to believe the facts unless we witness them. Also, if at all Kaushal was right about finding the transmitter in Richa's locker there might be a possibility that someone was trying to frame her.

There were just too many questions popping out of my head at that time. But this surely wasn't a time to ponder upon them. I pocketed the phone and headed towards the kitchen area. I soon took a bottle of water and rushed for the lawn.

By the time I reached the lawn, almost about everyone were beside Karan providing him shelter and giving him artificial air by waving their napkins and handkerchiefs around him.

"Here take this." I said handing over the bottle to Karan.

He drank it and slowly got up. The doctor was already there.

"I guess it's because of the afternoon Sun. Just rest for a

couple of hours and have some lime juice or a glucose drink."
he said.

Karan nodded as everyone began to disperse. The doctor
helped Karan walk towards our room where he could rest now,
even though he was perfectly fine. 'What a plan Karan' I thought
as I smiled inside.

Now all I needed was some time where I could hand the
phone over to Kaushal without anyone knowing. And most
importantly, without Richa realizing that it was missing from her
locker. Also, I had to place it back in there before the dinner
session ended as that is when she would check her locker again.
For all of this, I had only about 5-6 hours.

CHAPTER SIXTEEN

"Here you are sir." I said as I handed over Richa's cell-phone to Kaushal.

It was about 4.30 p.m the same day as I managed to grab the phone from Richa's locker, thanks to Karan.

"Good, my boy." Kaushal took it from me and examined the piece, "It's not even a camera phone, strange."

"Exactly, Sir. She is just too young and innocent to manage any spy operation or anything of that sort."

"We need to be sure, boy. Of course if she is innocent she has nothing to fear. In that case, we need to find out who is trying to frame her."

I nodded. Someone here was guilty for sure. Unfortunately Richa was being a scapegoat. But that is what I thought. The authorities needed to be sure of fact too.

'After today all this will end' I assured myself, 'Richa will be proven innocent and they will finally trace their investigation further eventually getting the real culprit.'

"Thomas!" Kaushal called out as Thomas came from behind his office, "Quick, check this device for bugs."

He handed the phone over to Thomas. Kaushal then noticed

my puzzled expression.

"Ohh.. You know Thomas right?" He said

I smiled as Thomas waved a 'hi' to me with his left hand as he took the phone from Kaushal.

"I mean you know him, but probably not the same way that you do now." Kaushal spoke further, "He works for us. We have our agents in here too, as students. Part of a security plan."

I was surprised. These people did really take the security issue much seriously than I thought they did.

"Okay you can leave now boy." Kaushal smiled as he asked me to leave the room.

"You have to understand something here Sir." I spoke, "I need to keep that thing back where it belongs before Richa finds out."

"Of course I understand. In about an hour or so we will be done with the examining with it for suspicious material or links regarding the device and you can take it back."

"Regarding the device? Isn't she clearly innocent after you find out that it's just a normal phone or are the links indeed nowhere headed to any anti-social organization?"

"Based solely on the phone examination? You wish, Boy." Kaushal walked towards me, "This is a serious case. We will examine the device, the contacts fed in it. We'll enquire further into the matter as time goes on. But one thing is for sure, if the phone device and its contacts don't lead us to anything suspicious, your friend won't be on our suspects list as the prime suspect. But surely we will be on the lookout though. Boy, no investigative agencies take decisions or make conclusions based on only single evidence. But this will certainly take the spotlight a bit away from her and you. Thomas is a technical expert in electronic devices; he will do his job and let us know. Till then it's too early to say anything."

I got his point. It would be stupid on behalf of any investigation agency to conclude anything based on single evidence. But this could prove to be a mammoth step in relaxing their eye on Richa.

"But then when can I take back the phone?" I asked as I saw Thomas had already begun with his work of clicking a few buttons and searching through the phone. Later he would be dismantling it, I guessed.

"Anytime after 2 hours from now." Kaushal said, "Don't worry, she won't know a thing. You people are allowed to check your lockers only after dinner now so you have more than enough time to take this back from us and place it where it belongs."

I nodded. "I just pray she does not try and access her locker before that." I said.

"Why would she? It isn't allowed." Kaushal said.

"Sir, students aren't even allowed to sneak out from the camp and bunk lectures, but we did right? I cannot guarantee anything from Richa. So please if you could make it fast."

"You've spoken too much." Kaushal wasn't used to being given an advice, "You may leave."

❈ ❈ ❈

About 5.30pm and we were in our Class-4 for our on-going lecture '*Where is God*'

Mrs. Nair, a forty-ish looking women took the lecture.

"So tell me. Where do you think God lives?" She asked.

I wondered why all their lectures at this workshop started with a question thrown at the audience. Probably it's a tact every successful presenter uses to know his audience better and get a gist of what to expect and what to give.

There was the usual buzzing and a couple of raised hands on the question.

"Well that question depends on other question; which is, whether God exists at all" someone spoke from the back.

"Oh, so we have an atheist in the class. Interesting." the teacher said.

Some more buzzing.

"So why it is so hard to believe that there is any God? Well that debate isn't our point of discussion over here. Not in this lecture at least."

I glanced around the class. I was sitting on the second last bench. Richa sat diagonally opposite to me in the neighboring row. Karan was in his room, taking rest for the day, as suggested by the doctor.

"So students, the thing is, the very concept of God is misunderstood in our society." Mrs. Nair continued, "What I mean here is that God has been described to us in various forms in various religions, but unfortunately we've mistaken His identity as the world progressed. God is nothing but a feeling. There is no one controlling anything in the universe. Everything happens because we make or do not make it happen. Our brain is just programmed to act like there is some actual physical entity to control us, when actually there nothing but a feeling!"

"Ma'm , you mean to say that God doesn't exist?" A person in a turban asked.

"Did I not say that it is a feeling? If there was God, and all he believed was in the well being of people and stuff, there would be no tragedy or anything unfair happening in the entire universe. God is there, but not in the form that we were told he is. It's just good people and their good deeds. You want to be close to God, you do good deeds. The feeling and the satisfaction you'll get after doing so, is God."

The class was listening silently now. Nair continued.

"Now tell me, you go to a religious place and say to God *'Please do so and so thing for me and I will offer you so and so money, or so and so jewels or gold or like 101 coconuts'*. How many of you do that?"

Not a single student raised his hand.

Mrs. Nair smiled as she said, "Well, now you're ashamed of admitting it, but at some time in life we all try and bribe the

Almighty. There are times when we promise God to behave well if we clear that critical paper or if we make it into the college of our choice after the entrance exam."

There was giggle in the class giving the indirect acceptance of the fact to Mrs. Nair. We all had done it at some point of time. They agreed with their collectively positive giggles.

"So tell me students, this God of yours' if at all he is a real powerful entity and has created an entire universe, would your offering of gold, or 101 coconuts do him any good?"

The students were getting the point.

"Wouldn't he be happier if you helped someone with that money or fed a poor child in his world rather than offering Him who has everything? The thing is, you are offering God what he himself has made for you! Isn't that a paradox?" She stopped.

There was clapping in the class. I had never seen anyone discuss God with such brief and yet simple but powerful explanation. The conversation in the class had just got interesting, when a peon entered the class and handed over a note to Mrs. Nair.

She opened the note as she announced "Vishal Rajguru?"

I stood up, "That's me ma'm."

"You have been called in the Deans' office right now."

I was surprised with the abrupt call for me. I didn't show surprise though and walked away with the peon.

From the corridors of the building to the office was about a 3 minute walk. But it felt like ages. These distances I tell you, are not measured in meters or miles only, they are also measured in mind-minutes, and thoughts per second is how you cut it.

Soon I entered the office. Kaushal was seated on his chair smiling at me. In front of him I saw Richa's cell-phone on the table.

"Welcome boy." he greeted me with a smile as he picked up the 'digital-distraction' in his hand and raised it at me, "Here take this back and keep it in her locker."

"So did you find anything?" I was more concerned than curious.

"I wouldn't share with you the entire thing, as it is against our policy and the investigation isn't over yet. But then on the first look of it, the phone seemed to be entirely normal to us, until we checked the saved contacts in it."

"What did you find Sir?"

"Nothing."

"What?"

"Yes, boy. Not a single contact saved. Neither in sim-card, nor in the phone memory. Not even a single sms."

"But that's a good thing or not?" I asked, "What does it prove?"

"You tell me boy, this teenage girl has a cell-phone with her, she is away from her home in a camp for like 14 days and she has not a single contact number saved in it? Not a single sms too? Who does that?"

I had to agree. This was strange.

"This is just what the secret agents or spies do! They always memorize the numbers and delete every call log and sms shared with their bosses or colleagues." Kaushal concluded.

"What else did you find Sir?"

"I think for the time being this much information is enough for you to know. We'll carry forward from here. Now you can replace her phone back to in the place where it was and we will let you know further developments as and when they come. We did not find anything fishy other than this fact that I told you regarding the contact numbers in the phone. But we sure have an eye on here."

"Sure sir." I said as I took the phone from Kaushal and began walking toward the door.

"And yes, if she or anyone asks you about why were you abruptly called into the office from the class then tell that it was regarding your documentary formalities and signing of some important documents in that regard." Kaushal said

"Yes sir, sure"

I now walked towards the lockers.

This was the safest time I could replace the phone back to the place from where I had picked it.

I reached the locker as I used my master key once again to open Richa's locker door.

'Sorry Richa, but I did this for you. You have something to hide after all it seems. I just wish whatever it is you should have shared with me' I thought.

I then thought of the box Richa had handed me. I wondered if opening that would provide me with the answers to the mindboggling questions I had right now. But I myself didn't know the password to it. This was one of the most bizarre situations one can possibly be. It was like you have been handed over a lock as present without the key. Too many questions. I always knew this girl was special, weird and adventurous, but not in such a way. Not in a bad way.

Of course there must be some valid explanation to all this.

I then put my right hand in my jeans pocket as I reached out for the phone. I placed it right back from where I had picked it in the afternoon and locked the door back.

I closed my eyes and prayed for everything to be alright and forgive me if at all I had done anything wrong to God. But wait, as Mrs Nair said, God was just a feeling. If that's true, then that feeling was missing right now.

Just then I felt someone breathing behind close to me. Someone was standing right behind me watching me place the phone in the locker all this time! I should've been careful and not take it for granted that even there was a class going on, no one would come here.

I gathered some courage as I turned back swiftly to see who it was. About less than a foot behind me stood Richa staring at me. Her eyes were watery but she didn't blink.

"I-I... can..." I started to explain

Richa stopped me as she said, "Please don't! So it was you!"

CHAPTER SEVENTEEN

Earlier that day,
Before Mrs. Nair's Lecture.
Few hours ago

"You need to let it out, man." Richa said as we walked towards our class.

"Let out what?" I asked her.

"Whatever that's freaking the hell out of you right now." She shot back.

"Well, I'm not freaking out!" I defended myself yet again.

"No matter how much you try man, you can't hide anything nor can carry on with a lie smoothly. You've been acting weird for quite a while now. What's bothering you?"

"Nothing." I said without looking at her. I wanted to avoid as much eye contact as I could.

I just prayed hard that no matter what, she didn't check her locker for her phone. Not at least for the next few hours until I get it back from Kaushal.

"Okay. Don't tell me." Richa said as she began walking faster than me now.

I doubled my speed to keep up with her.

"There's nothing to hide Richa!" I told her.

She stopped suddenly. I stopped too.

She then held me by my shirt collar using both her hands and pushed me towards the wall of the corridor.

"Tell me, is it about the box? Did you tell anyone?" she whispered.

"NO! I would never do that!" I replied. For once, I wasn't lying to her.

"Are you nervous?"

"About?"

"About the box, *dumbo*! Is that what is eating up your head?"

I thought for a second, "Oh yes, yes, that's exactly why I'm nervous. I'm very much curious and nervous about the box and whatever message that box contains. That is the exact reason why I'm so weird and all." I blurted out.

'Perfect' , I thought, 'Why didn't I think of this earlier!'

"Well, as I told you, just forget that there's any box. That box actually contains nothing but a secret number which I'm supposed to use only when there's no other way of getting out." Richa loosened the collar of my shirt.

"Getting out of what?"

"That's not important."

"Then why did you give it to me?"

"See, now that we're together there is a slight possibility that you might be involved in this at some point. This is just in case we need a back up. Just in case YOU need a backup."

"Then why the secret box drama! You could've told me straight away."

"No, letting out a secret without being sure if it will be used for a good deed is not right. I had to give it to you, but also need to make sure that you won't be in a position to exploit it in a wrong way until you really really needed it."

"And by not telling me the code to the box, you know I won't be able to use it?"

"Yes."

"And what about when I'll actually really really need it!"

"Then, you'll know what to do."

"HOW?"

"Enough, let's get to the class."

I hated how Richa always chose to keep the best of the answers to her.

I without much ado now, started following her.

And just before we entered the class, Richa turned back and said, "And yes Vishy, here's a thing."

"What?"

"Don't ever try and lie to me. Because you can't."

"What do you mean?"

"I mean I know you're curious about the box and all, but it isn't that box that's making you go all crazy around since yesterday. You may choose to hide your secrets from me, but never lie."

She finished her sentence and walked away.

I stood there for a couple of seconds. I wasn't sure what to do. The girl just read me too well.

Either I needed to learn to lie efficiently, or just get away by telling her the truth. But in the current situation, neither of them were a possible option for me.

CHAPTER EIGHTEEN

Present time,
At the lockers

About just 10 minutes after Richa had caught me red-handed we were in the corner of the corridor. Richa pushed me against the wall and demanded a suitable explanation.

Ever seen that movie scene where the thief is caught, but not while stealing; instead, he's caught while keeping those things back where they belonged! Hilarious they seem. I felt like that exactly right now, with a difference, there was nothing to laugh at.

"So do you want to share with me what all is going on here?" Richa asked.

"Did you share everything with me Richa in the first place?" I shot back; I was prepared with my defense.

Richa gave me a puzzled look.

"Those things you were looking for the other day weren't your earrings were they?" I asked looking straight into her eyes. I had the feeling that now that she demanded some answers from me it was my time too to get some from her. The sharing and trust, if any, had to be two-way.

"You don't know what you are doing Vishal, you will just have to trust me!" Richa said holding my hand in both of hers.

"Trust is two-way Richa. I understand your situation here totally, but I need to know what is going on here, what you are up to."

"I have no idea what you were doing near my locker. But I trust you enough to know that you'd never do anything harmful to me." Richa said, "You'll have to come up with an open mind and share with me whatever that's bothering you Vishal."

"I need some answers first." I said, "Trust should be mutual. Even though I'm not supposed to share much with you, I guess I know you well enough to break some rules. Can I trust you Richa?"

"Okay. I'll tell you everything, I trust you." Richa said finally, "Anyways I was going to tell you soon. I need some help from you."

"Then you should've asked for it straight away!"

"No. I needed to win your trust and confidence. This is deeper than it seems, remember the greater purpose?"

I nodded.

"Okay let's disperse right now." Richa said, "I excused myself from the class saying that I needed to use the restroom. We'll head back to the class one after the other as if this never happened. And later at dinner, I will tell you everything you need to know about this."

I agreed. Even though I had too many questions left unanswered by Richa, We couldn't risk being caught together. The authorities should be kept in the dark about Richa finding out that we have been keeping her on a watch now.

Finally it was 8.30 in the evening and dinner time. Karan was still in our room and his dinner was served there by the helpers of the workshop. Richa and I helped ourselves with our dinner plates and went on to the seat in the corner of dinner hall. I didn't care about any of the authorities seeing us together or chat, because they themselves had told me to behave normal by with Richa so that she did not know about us spying on her activities. What they did not know as of now was that Richa knew that they were actually spying, through me. Too much of confusion. It was time to clear it all, I thought.

"So tell me what this was all about.?" Richa asked me

"You start first." I demanded, "You know what they found in your locker when we had gone for our little misadventure."

Richa looked at me puzzled.

"A transmitter!"

Richa smiled as she looked down at her plate as she said, "These people aren't as good in practicality when it comes to spying and stuff as they seemed."

"You mean…"

"I mean it wasn't a transmitter" Richa continued, "It was an advanced sound recording device."

"So you do agree!" I was surprised.

"Yes. When did I deny it?" Richa was calm.

"I don't know what to say Richa! What are you doing with these smart spy devices here in the workshop? Who are you?"

"Relax." Richa said, "First tell me, what they told you?"

In the next three minutes or so I narrated the entire conversation between Kaushal and me word to word, to which she calmly gave a keen ear. Wasn't sure if I was doing the right thing while blurting it out to her, but my heart told me it was. The heart always won when it came to decision making. But it wasn't always right.

"And you believed him?" She asked after I finished.

"Did I have an option?" I answered, "To start with, you had all your form filled without the signatures and stuff, and then the details were forged. To add to it, I had broken the rules of this workshop by running away from it for like a day and had signed your papers as a guardian, remember? Further investigation or problems would be diverted to me in case you run away or do something terrible!"

Richa kept quiet. She understood the situation well.

"Well, don't worry. Everything will be alright." She said

I hoped it had better be.

"Ever heard of sting operations or investigative journalism?"
Richa asked me.

"Of course I have, you mean the *Tehelka* types?" I asked back.

Richa nodded a 'yes'. "So I'm one of those." She added.

"What? So all you are doing here is carrying out a sting
operation?" I didn't know what to believe.

"Yes." Richa said, "Let's start from the beginning, may I?"

"Go ahead, my head is already spinning." I said.

She then began with her story:

"Actually, I'm Richa Dixit, not Richa Rao. I'm a journalist.
Heard of the *The New Times*?"

"Of course, it is the number three newspaper and making way
to the top spot considering the quality of investigative journalism
it does, with the stings done on the recent scams in the city!" I
answered.

"Yes, I am hired by those people." Richa smiled, "But as an
intern. I'm on this assignment here and if I get them even one
concrete vital clue then I will be the youngest one to get hired as
one of their honorable team of journalists!"

"Vital clue? Of what?" I asked.

"See there was this report in our newspaper about a year
back that since this *A Way Around* has gone international; there
have several un-confirmed reports of some suspicious activities
being carried out in the workshop."

"Suspicious? You mean?"

"Drug trafficking." she said plainly.

"No! You know what you are saying aren't you!" I was taken
aback by this statement of hers.

"I did say its un-confirmed report didn't I? Anyways, we did
alert the Government regarding our findings from the sources

but they needed concrete proof and dismissed our claim back then. All of a sudden, the workshop made a decision of banning all the digital-distractions inside their premises until the course of 14 day was over. Co-incidence? No."

"So you mean to say they did not have this policy of not allowing cell-phones, cameras and stuff before your report was submitted to the government?"

"No, it happened as soon as we did it. They were surely hiding something and banned every other digital device on the campus as a clause in their policy to avoid any sting as the word was spreading regarding our report, which they termed as rumors. We couldn't do anything but get proof which wasn't possible without some technical help or co-operation from the Government. Our biggest fear is that a part of the Government, that is the some of the top notch Ministers are involved too."

"I don't believe this!" I said.

"See, why is it so unbelievable? The workshop people travel to countries in the name of this workshop thing; they need clearance from the Government to conduct courses outside the country. We complain against them about our doubts and findings, the Government dismiss it. Moreover immediately strange rules in the name of 'policy' are being made in the Workshop, which when reported to the Ministers or authorities in the Government in charge, we get a reply *'It's an independent private organization and Government has nothing to do with it. We cannot fiddle with the rules that they make'*"

I listened. I felt as if I was in a bad dream and soon Karan would splash water on my face or kick me to wake me up. But it wasn't, Richa went on:

"As time passed, *A Way Around's* screening process toughened. Every suspicious candidate's backgrounds were being checked in fear of getting exposed. Only the common man and innocent students admitted, trained for 14 days and then left. No suspicious government employee or media person was admitted and his application was being refused under the violation of some rules & regulations. This is an activity workshop on paper, but inside there's a much bigger illegal activities going on. Drug trafficking is just one of them. They get an easy clearance in almost all the European and some other countries in the name of the workshop. And through this they conduct a 14 day workshop wherever they want with some of their agents acting as students there and doing their usual trafficking things. We aren't sure if that's all they do. But this one is for sure, we aren't getting any help from the Government and we had to do this on our own."

"So you running this expose operation on them?" I asked.

"See, last one year one journo tried to get into this workshop. But these people did research pretty well in advance and somehow kept trouble away by rejecting the forms of 'possible threats' saying the seats were full or by finding some clause that they had violated their terms and conditions. Only the 'safest students' from the application database were selected for the workshop. It has been observed that the forms that got short listed for the last one year or so were only of students below twenty one and people who had already retired. That way it ensured that these people did not belong to any one, they were just plain harmless people."

"How could they be so sure?" I asked

"Well they could never be, and they know it too! But it's a precaution. And even if someone sneaked in, there is no possible way he or she could investigate and gather hardcore evidence on the same in the limited period of 14 days that too without any digital equipment. Plus, not even mere cell phones are allowed simply meant no communication with the outside world while the workshop was on. They've tried their best to prevent any possible sting. Even if any person does find anything in here, how does he prove it to the outside world? No way."

Slowly, step by step Richa was making some sense to me.

"So then these *The New Times* group of investigative journos needed a new face for this sting. Someone who had never worked for them so that the world and by that I mean *A Way Around* would never know. I had given an interview for a position as an intern there, then I was suddenly offered this assignment. Now who gets such an opportunity on the first day of the job!"

I nodded, she continued.

"Also, our agency had done their home work and found out that this time a student had been finally allowed with his digital distractions such as camera and stuff. We saw it as the best opportunity to get some real evidence if our infiltration in the camp was made exactly when you were here. I was told to be friends with that student, that means you, and use your luxuries to get some hard hitting evidence!"

"But then why would they allow me with my camera and all in? Didn't they see me as a potential threat?" I asked.

"No. As I said, they must've researched pretty well on you and your background and then only allowed you with such luxury. Also, giving out themselves openly to a documentary might also send positive signals to the critics outside."

I nodded. It made sense.

"Oh so this was what it was all about?" I asked.

"I didn't even know who you were. You were just a source of my digital equipments to capture evidences at first. I was to use you to capture what I thought was as an evidence. But it was like a sign from God, that I had forgot to sign my own documents and who else than you to come to the rescue. The moment you announced your name in the cabin there to Ms. Puja, it struck me that it was you who I supposed to befriend and God had made it easier for me as you yourself had approached me, rather than the other way round!"

I was listening.

"But this wasn't it." Richa continued, "It had started well but I had to win your confidence and test the extent to which you would co-operate with me, hence that escape adventure thing.

That was just to test you how much you blind-trusted me. After that day you weren't just a resource for me. As I got to know you better, you become a special friend."

"And when were you actually planning to tell me about your real intentions of the sting over here?" I asked

"I was going to today, but then things got ugly and my AVR got stolen from the locker, which I was supposed to hand over to you after telling my real story and that you would keep it where I wanted it to collect evidence! With you having a license to roam about almost freely with that digital camera of yours for your documentary thing, no one would suspect you even if you were seen at places when student's do not visit that often."

No wonder this girl had a plan for every problem. Whatever newspaper this girl worked for or at least that's what she said, had brilliantly laid plan. Use my luxury as their investigating and recording tools. Use my access and license to roam about anywhere as their means to go through scanning the workshop. Along with my documentary they wanted a parallel sting to be carried out!

"Vishy" Richa said as she placed her palms on my shoulder, "If this hadn't taken an ugly turn, I would anyways have told you everything and we would be in this together. You believe me don't you?"

"How do I know Richa?" I was even more confused, "That Kaushal and you are blaming each other. You both plead that the other is guilty! I guess it's time for the police to take over. Whosoever is innocent has nothing to fear right?"

"You are dead wrong Vishy," Richa said shaking her head, "Did I not say that this racket is bigger than it seems? Every top notch authority is involved. We cannot approach anyone without hard evidence! No one will believe us. On the contrary I would be punished for submitting forged documents and you would be punished for helping in a forgery! They would frame us somehow to get rid of us. Calling in the cops would be utterly stupid and warn them in advance."

She was making sense.

"But then how do I decide which side to take!" I said

"No side." Richa answered, "Now that you had taken my mobile phone to them and done your part of investigation for them, now do what I tell you. If I can prove it to you that they are in fact guilty then what's the problem? You did what they said. Now do what I say, and decide for yourself. I'm not even asking you to trust me blindly."

She deserved a fair trial too. I had listened to whatever Kaushal had said and this was Richa. Also, she wasn't asking anything absurd. All she said was to do whatever she said and then make my decision.

"Fair enough, what do I have to do?"

"Great!" Richa said as she hugged me tightly, "I'll tell you what to do. Let's finish dinner first."

I watched as after this whole confrontation and explanation thing, she merrily chomped on her food.

Man, what was this girl really made of! Did she even have any feelings like anxiety, nervousness, or fear? I virtually saluted her for her calm and presence of mind and continued with my dinner.

CHAPTER NINETEEN

It was after dinner that Richa and I walked up to my room where Karan too had finished his dinner that was served to him there as he was advised rest by the physio for the day.

"So buddy how you feeling?" I asked him as we entered and winked at Karan.

"Yeah I'm well now." Karan said in a less feeble voice than in the afternoon. He was a damn good actor. He winked back at me just when Richa wasn't watching either of us.

Richa still had no idea that Karan's collapse in the afternoon on the ground was just to create a distraction so that I could keep her cell phone back in the locker.

"You seem better than in the morning of course and by tomorrow you'll be back with us." Richa smiled as she checked his temperature by placing her hand on his forehead.

"Okay let him take rest, Vishal." Richa said turning back to me, "And we will go take a round or two in the lawn before we go to sleep"

I nodded, switched off the tube light in the room and walked behind Richa to the lawn.

"Now tell me, what are we supposed to do?" I asked Richa as

we started walking around the lawn.

"We'll just play as they wanted to play it. You know that I know, but they don't know that I know." She said, "So you just go on doing what they say to you, or at least pretend to do so and also work for me. That way, they would never suspect you of doing anything suspicious. You gather clues or whatever for both of us and make your own decision based on them!"

"Fair enough." I said, "But what exactly and where am I supposed to look for what you say could be your evidence in proving the workshop's guilt?"

"See, that's what I came here to investigate about! You have more access and authority to roam about in here more than anyone and that too with the camera and stuff!"

I had to agree. It was like a free walk. Earlier I had to acquire permission from the authorities to take photographs or video film in any part of the workshop or lecture. But now that I worked for them and had gained their confidence by handing over my friends' cell-phone to them they would have no problem with me roaming around freely. This way I could pretend doing my documentary thing and gather 'evidences' if any as suggested by Richa.

I saw no harm in doing such a thing. Because none of the parties were forcing their belief on to me. I was just told to search and look for clues, find them if any and make a decision. That's it. The rest would be handled by the Government and police agencies as the clues were gathered.

Easier said than done.

"So where do we start?" I asked Richa

"Okay, do you know any place here which you haven't seen? Or let's say a place which usually no student or staff members use?"

I thought for a minute.

"Yes, there's this small store-room, filled with boxes and locked cupboard near the kitchen floor where I had been while filming with Mr. Iyer."

"Good." Richa gave it a thought as she continued, "And strangely enough, all the classes are held on the ground floor even though there are two more rooms that could be used as classrooms above on the kitchen level, which in fact seem to be more spacious and well ventilated."

I had to agree. There were two huge hall-like rooms upstairs but were kept locked. Maybe the authorities just wanted to keep everyone away from that store room. I wasn't sure as on second thoughts it could might as well have been a mere co-incidence.

At times our mind related every possible details of the current situation to something we wanted to believe in.

"So when you were there, did you see anything suspicious?" Richa questioned me

"No, actually at that time I wasn't even looking for anything. I was there briefly, from the time Iyer took me there to the time Kaushal entered. Then he took over the conversation." I said.

"I think the store room could be our first place to explore." Richa said, "At least until we get our next lead."

"Yes, but what are we looking for in there?"

"Any documents that you might stumble on. If it was a store room and some illegal activity was going on here like drug trafficking, there would thousands of things you would need to maintain and forge. Fake IDs , fake passports, forms etc." Richa said, "Basically look for any set of documents or anything else in there, click pictures, take videos and we'll see later what we can make out of them. Of course there's no possibility of any drugs or anti-social-items that you'll find there."

"But how will I get in?" I asked.

"*Dumbo* you are!" Richa mocked me again, "Don't you have that master key that you used to open my locker?"

"But that was meant for your locker!"

"It's a master key my darling! Not a duplicate key. I guess it would work on any locker or any lock in here. Technically it should, worth a try."

I nodded. Sometimes you couldn't just match such fast thinking of certain people.

"Also one more thing." Richa said.

"What is that?"

"You'll have to do it when there is absolutely no chance of anyone being near the kitchen area. We cannot risk anyone seeing you snooping in there. You understand? For other places you can choose your own time of the day, but this store room is a sensitive place! You just have to do it when you're absolutely sure about no one even coming near that place."

"Hmm.." I went into a thinking mode, "Early morning can't be a good option as the breakfast preparations start well around 5 am and from then till the lunch the chefs and other kitchen people are constantly on rounds for something or the other."

"Yes, also after lunch the evening snacks preparations or tea/ coffee stuff goes on and eventually the preparation for dinner starts." Richa concluded.

"Then what do we do?"

"Well I know of a time when no one would be accessing that area" Richa said

"And when is that?" I asked

"Maybe between 2 and 4?"

"But you mentioned that after lunch they immediately start preparing snacks and–." I was stopped by Richa.

"I meant A.M." She whispered, "2 to 4 a.m."

CHAPTER TWENTY

Day 7
2.10 A. M

I glanced at the wrist watch kept on the table right next to me. It read 2.10a.m.

I was awake for the last 3 or 4 hours so that I could finish what I had started; what Richa had told me to do. I glanced at the bed right opposite to me. Karan was snoring. It was pitch dark outside and the entire building was calm and everything outside was motionless except the noises made by some night bugs outside. The moonlight was the only source of light in the room making its way through the window, playing hide and seek with the window curtains as it fluttered due the occasional breeze.

I rose from the bed. Wore my *chappals*, but then removed them again after thinking for a while. I did not want to make any noise. Not even the slightest one. I picked up my digital camera (and not the handy-cam) for obvious reasons that the former one could be easily concealed & kept in the trouser pocket. I did not even know whether I would even need it or not. I had no idea whether I was going to collect the evidence or just capture its image in my camera. I was thinking too far ahead, as to start with, I even didn't know what I was looking for. I didn't know what my evidence would be. I was just told by Richa to look for anything suspicious. Any documents, a physical evidence, anything. Anything that I thought should not have been there and seemed out of place.

I walked out of the room making my way down the long corridor. It was pitch dark outside. Not even the moonlight in the corridors. But my eyes were accustomed to the darkness by now. I walked carefully as I could see the faint staircases that led up to the kitchen and store room area.

I stopped for a moment to take a deep breath.

'This is it' I told myself and began walking again.

I climbed the stairs. One step at a time. When you're anxious about something, they say time runs slow and a minute seems like an hour. Right now, I felt each step as a staircase of 100 steps. Finally after a couple of more seconds in the common world and hours in my mind I made it right in front of the store room door. I reached for the master key in my trouser pocket and inserted it into the lock. Within a couple of rounds of twisting, turning and fidgeting with the lock, the door creaked open.

I wished Richa was with me tonight. She made everything seem simple and easy. Or maybe her presence was what made me feel stronger than I was. I didn't know what it was, but all I wished was that if only she could be here right now.

"It would be too risky Vishy," She had told me when I had asked her, "More the people, more the movement, plus they keep a watch on me already. I fear that some of them might be watching my room all night. You'll have to do this all by yourself."

I took another deep breath as I entered the store room. It was dusty and I got a feeling of letting out an instant sneeze but somehow managed to control it.

As soon as I entered the room I turned back and closed the door behind me. I reached for the small dim bulb button on the wall and switched it on. It flickered before it lit the room with a light so dim that the moonlight in our room seemed much brighter. But good enough, as the last thing I wanted right now was a spotlight right on me.

I glanced around the entire room. I had been here the previous day of course, but then at that time I wasn't looking for anything. Now it was different. I was looking for any minutest thing that would serve as 'evidence'.

I glanced up at the cupboards in the room. These cupboards did not have the usual in-built lock but were traditional with a hanging lock, waiting to be opened. I glanced at my master-key, hoped for the best and inserted it in one of the three of those cupboards. I twisted and turned the key for about a few times. The lock refused to open. I tried again. Nothing.

I was about to give up after just one last try and then the lock cracked open.

'My goodness, it worked' I thought. A cold shiver ran through my spine even before opening the cupboard in the mere anxiousness that what I would find in it. I then gathered enough courage to open the lock completely and with a swing action opened the door.

A cloud of dust flew off before the doors opened.

'This might not have been in use for years!' I thought.

I glanced inside the cupboard. It was empty.

I then went on to the next cupboard. Equally dusty and empty too. It seemed that I was at a dead end and for the first time I felt that Richa wasn't quite right. But it was too soon to jump on to a conclusion. I had to be sure, dead sure.

I moved towards the last cupboard. Unlike the other two, it was relatively clean.

This indicated something. Yes. It was in use! The third cupboard was being used to store something and hence wasn't as dusty or rusty as the other two. A sense of excitement mixed with some anxiousness and fear filled me as I inserted the key into its lock. My excitement died the moment I attempted to open the lock for the third cupboard.

The key did not even manage to make it halfway and got stuck in between. I observed the lock. It was different. The lock to the third cupboard was clearly different from the type that the first two had! Obviously, there was something valuable in there!

I stood for about half a minute staring at the lock thinking, 'C'mon, tell me how I get you to open!' Unfortunately locks don't speak nor do they reveal. That isn't what they are made for in the first place. I grabbed my digital camera from my trouser and took a couple of pictures of the cupboard and a close-up snap of the lock. I don't know why I did that. But I did.

I glanced around. There were those huge cardboard boxes piled up one on another at a corner. They weren't even sealed. I thought I might as well take a look at what it held. The box was huge enough, such that when full, it would take at least two people to lift it off the ground. I went near one of the boxes, which was piled up on another one and opened one of its two flaps.

Nothing.

I picked up the empty box and kept it aside as I turned open the flap of the box beneath it. This one surely wasn't empty. It had some documents. My eyes lighted up suddenly. Finally there was something that I could look into now. There were a couple of old admission forms and other documents related to some official paper work from past year.

'Not of much help' I thought, 'Obviously, all off the important stuff was right there in the cupboard number 3, right in front of me but I was unable access it.'

I shuffled the documents upside-down to search for something that seemed important or suspicious. Nothing again.

Just then I heard something. Initially I thought if it was a rat or some animal sneaked into the store room. But that wasn't the case. The noise came from outside the store room.

The noise was that of the footsteps climbing up the stairs! By the sound of the footsteps it was quite clear that there was more than one person approaching the store room.

I panicked for a moment.

I glanced to the left and right of the room. There was no place I could hide. It being a simple store-room had no place to hide! I looked at the two cupboards I had opened. I quickly locked them back. For once I had thought of hiding in one of them, but it would've been a really bad idea. With the amount of dust and dirt in there, I would surely have sneezed or coughed or suffocated if not anything. Also, I being inside would mean no lock from the outside. Bad idea.

The only place I could hide now was one of the huge cardboard boxes.

It was a lame idea, but still I had to try as there was nowhere else to go. I did not want to stand in the middle of the store room at 2.30a.m and surprise the visitors. I knew I would get caught eventually but it was worth a try than giving up easily.

The footsteps approached nearer, I quickly ran towards the dim light switch. I turned it off and ran towards the box I had just opened and climbed into it. I curled myself inside it like an earthworm in the soil and took over the flaps of it to cover the top.

The visitors had reached up to the door now, which obviously, wasn't locked from outside! This situation would make even the dumbest person on the earth understand that there was an infiltration! My little fantasy of escaping the scenario by hiding in this box was clearly coming to an end.

CHAPTER TWENTY ONE

"How's the lock open?" a familiar voice asked his fellow visitor while both still stood outside the door of the store room.

"No idea sir, we might have forgotten to close it in a hurry."

"You idiot! How can you even think of giving such an excuse! Did I not tell you that she is here and we need to be even more careful now?"

"But the boy is on our side, right? He'll take care of it sir."

"We can never trust anyone. He is on our side alright, but we never know for how long that will continue."

"Yes, but don't worry sir, I just checked, she's fast asleep in her room. I had Thomas keep a watch on her room yesterday too. She never visited this place."

Even though the door was closed and I was inside the box, I could make out every single word of what they spoke; for two reasons, one – it being past 2.30 a.m. there was deafening silence in the entire building and the only voices I could hear were of those two who stood behind an unlocked door about a few feet away, and two – they spoke normally rather than choosing to speak in whispers, which I found strange. I assumed that the girl they mentioned in their conversation was Richa and the boy was obviously me. The brief conversation made it very clear for any sane person to understand that they surely were up to something and trying to hide it. They knew who Richa was and were well aware of the threat she posed to them in some way or the other.

"Okay now enough, get in!" the familiar voice said as the door opened.

By now I was sure who that familiar voice belonged to. It was Kaushal. The other voice I had heard for the first time. Must be one of the peons or helpers.

Then the light was turned on. A ray of dim light entered the box through the flap. The two visitors were inside the room now. My hands began to shiver like hell.

Through the slight edges of the flaps of the box I tried to peep out to catch a glimpse of what they were up to, but couldn't see anything. So I decided to keep quiet and try and make sense out of the movement and their conversation to know more.

"Okay now open it."

"Yes sir."

There was a noise which indicated that a lock was being opened. It must surely have been the third cupboard. The one in which they were hiding something. Possibly another one of their secrets, and what Richa called 'evidence'.

"Could you please lend a hand Sir? It's too..." the other voice said as it seemed that he was struggling to get some parcel into the cupboard, and it was heavy.

Kaushal made some noise as he helped the person with him. After a few small noises of the things getting placed on a cupboard shelf, Kaushal said, "Now enough, let's go."

I heard the cupboard door close and the lock was being placed again. Their secret was secure again. I couldn't believe my luck. I was hiding less than a couple of feet away from there in that box and they never seemed to notice!

'Close call' I thought to myself as the lights were turned off by the visitor.

I then heard the door being closed as both Kaushal and the other visitor yet again stood out of the store room door. I decided to stay in the box and come out only when I thought it was completely safe to do so.

"And what about the lock Sir?" I heard the other man ask Kaushal.

"Where's the previous one?"

"It wasn't here Sir, didn't we find the door open while we came here?"

"This is disgusting. you are So ignorant! Now go get another lock." Kaushal instructed.

"From where sir? It's 2.40a.m! Can we replace the lock in the morning?"

"No." Kaushal was adamant, "First things first. Go, for the time being get the kitchen door lock and place it here. We'll get another lock for the kitchen in the morning. We cannot risk this room unlocked now that we know she's here in our camp, even though we have an eye on her."

The other person went away for a while. I assumed that he must have gone to fetch the other lock. The original lock for the store room door was still in my pocket.

After a couple of minutes, the other person returned back as he spoke to Kaushal, "Here it is sir."

"Okay now put it on to the door. And underline this, we cannot and just cannot afford to be so careless henceforth!" Kaushal spoke in a stern voice.

Again I heard the noise of the key and lock playing with each other, and then a final click, it had successfully safeguarded the secret. Both locks had done their job, the one at the third cupboard and the one on the store room door.

And now something struck me. Sooner or later someone would come to open the door in the morning or evening and find me. I had nowhere to go now. I couldn't just possibly walk out of the room as it had a lock on the outside now, nor could I ask for help if Kaushal or any of the authorities ever came inside by opening the door because I had no good excuse to give them for the reason behind me being there.

The scenario was plain and simple. The lock to the store room was now replaced by the kitchen lock, from outside. I had the master key which could probably work, but I was on the wrong side of the door. In simple words, I was locked inside, forever.

CHAPTER TWENTY TWO

Approximately about half an hour had passed. Or even more maybe. I wasn't sure of the exact time. My joints and back had started to ache in the box. Now that enough time had passed inside the box, I thought it would be a good idea to get out of the compact box and stretch a bit. If not from Kaushal or any of the authority finding out about this, I would surely die of the body ache, it seemed.

I got myself outside the box slowly. My knee joints and back made slight cracking noises. I stood shakily on the floor. It was very hard to predict how much time I had been inside in the curled up 'earthworm-position' but it surely felt like an eternity. Maybe in the normal world it might have been just 15-20 minutes. I had experienced the Einstein's theory of relativity, which said precisely, *Go on a date with a beautiful young lady and 2 hours seem like a minute. Place your hand on a hot stove for a minute and it seems like an hour.* Right now, the box was my stove.

I then approached the cupboard number 3 and stared at the lock.

'If only stares could open it' I thought, 'What are they hiding really?'

I then moved towards the box again. I had nothing else to do than go through the documents in there in the dim light, which I had now switched on again. I couldn't get out as the door was locked from outside. When and how I would make it out of here safely was the only question that I was avoiding to think about.

I shuffled through the papers in the box again, trying to make sense of anything important. Then something caught my eye. Apart from all the previous year's forms and expired documents, I found a map. It was a simple print-out of a map of a certain area. It was hard to read the miniature landscapes and locations in the dim light, but I pocketed it by folding it into a few folds and keeping it in the trouser pocket. The rest was the same. Documents, forms and more documents. I was exhausted. I then gave up my search and just sat on the floor in the corner of the room by placing my back on the wall. It made me feel relaxed somehow.

About an hour passed again. I lay there sitting in the corner with my eyes closed. Approximately half an hour passed when I heard some noise again which made me open my eyes.

It was the sound of foots-steps again. I hurriedly got back into the box.

'What were they back for now?' I thought as I hid myself.

This time there was noise of footsteps of only one person. I wondered who it could be.

I anxiously waited as I heard the lock to the store room being opened. The person walked in and closed the door back as the dim light was turned on again.

"Vishal!" the person whispered, "Are you there? It's me!"

It was Richa! She had indeed come to rescue me!

I instantly came out of the box and saw her standing in the middle of the store room.

We looked at each other. I was surprised. She wasn't. I wonder what that one thing would be that would really shake her up from her ever-green calm and composed nature.

"How did you-." I began to ask her but she instantly signaled me to stay quiet.

"I'll explain *dumbo*! This isn't the time and place to do it." She whispered as she held my hand and dragged me to the door. She was right, this wasn't the time that she could explain me how she got to know I was trapped inside and how she managed to come here all by herself and open the lock.

Within minutes both of us were outside the store room. She put the lock back on to the door and then we left to our respective rooms.

CHAPTER TWENTY THREE

7.30a.m
Breakfast Time

"So tell me now." I said.

Richa, Karan and I were at one side of the lawn, with our breakfast once again, after our Yoga session. By now we had explained the entire situation to Karan who was surprised or shocked rather with the turn of events. He had the same expressions while listening to our story as a kid would have on his first roller-coaster ride. He had no clue whether to laugh, cry, yell or simply enjoy the ride.

"So tell me how you found out I was trapped and how did you managed to get the key of the lock." I asked Richa again.

She smiled. Karan was anxious to know the answer too.

"Obviously I knew you were in there as I had told you to go.. But regarding you being trapped I'll tell you." Richa began to narrate, "That Kaushal guy had kept a guy spying secretly on me the entire night as we had rightly guessed they would. I acted as if I hadn't noticed him and was fast asleep. About until 4 in the morning I had the feeling that I was being watched from a distance, and then suddenly I sensed someone leave the corridor.

I got up and peeped through the window and saw that my spy had gone away. It was 4.40a.m by then. Only on being sure that the coast was completely clear I tip-toed to your room to see if you were alright. You weren't there and Karan was snoring. I saw your *chappals* beside your bed. It was clear that you had gone for our 'mission'. I then decided to take a look at the store-room myself, and found you."

"And what about the store-room keys? Where did you get them?" Karan asked.

"I have my ways" Richa quipped. I wasn't sure what she meant by it.

"Duplicate keys? Another master key?" Karan asked again.

Richa shrugged and ignored the question.

"O my God. You have someone else in this workshop working with you other than Vishal, don't you?" Karan gasped.

The question shook me too. If what Karan thought was right, this was much deeper and more complex than it seemed. Richa decided to pass that question too as she said, "Okay now can we stop interrogating me and concentrate on what to do next?"

Karan and I nodded.

"So what did you find Vishy?" Richa asked pointing towards me.

Thankfully there was this little was thing about her that I couldn't ignore; she never called me with her usual '*dumbo*' name that she was fond of, in public. Not even when Karan was around. She referred to me as Vishy rather than her usual '*dumbo*'.

"Nothing actually." I said, "Except this piece of map, that I found lying in the dusty box kept un-sealed, everything seemed normal. The main stuff I guess is all stuffed in that main cupboard number 3, to which we have to get some access if we want to have some evidence."

"God damn Vishal, you got that paper with you!" Karan asked.

"It's a map."

"Whatever! But you should've taken a picture of it in your camera instead of getting the copy in here."

"He's right." Richa said, "They could find it missing and everything we are doing here without them knowing would make no sense."

"I know." I said, "But this piece of map, is worthless. If it had some value they would have stuffed in the cupboard all locked up. This one was lying there all by itself in the box."

"But then why did you bring it, if it were worthless?"

"Because, even though it might be worthless now, it might have been of some use in the past! It might help us, if not them."

Karan and Richa watched as I took out the piece of paper from my pocket and lay it on my lap for both of them to see it.

It was a map of some area, zoomed and printed out from the internet. Also it had 3 circles marked by a blue pen naming the points as A, B and C.

"This is the map of this area itself!" Richa pointed out.

She was right. The map was of the very city in which the workshop was being held. *Lonavala.*

The 3 locations marked on it were of a lodge, a rest house and a farmhouse all about 10-15 kms from the workshop site.

"There's something written behind" Karan pointed out.

I turned over the map as we all saw a hand written note saying:

A : 10th December
B : 14th December
C : 19th December

"What does this even mean?" Karan asked.

"A, B, C are the locations obviously that are marked on the map and the dates probably denote the events or tasks to be done there on those respective days?" I answered.

"I'm not sure what to guess from this" Richa said, "See, these circled places are just any normal semi luxury lodge, rest house and a farmhouse locations and I don't see a reason why these people would conduct any parallel event or activity in such place so close to the workshop."

"Then what could this mean?" Karan was still staring at the map.

"Maybe this is one of their store-rooms? Control room? Some place where they could just keep certain things which could not be kept here or those are too dangerous to be put over here?" I asked.

"Do you realize, today is 18th December." Karan spoke with an amount of excitement in his voice.

"So?"

"So, according to the map, tomorrow is an important day at Place C! Don't you see?"

"I'm not sure." Richa said.

"Why?"

"See, this map as you said, wasn't hidden and was lying there just by itself in the box so it wasn't of much value. I think it's too old and also, it does mention dates I agree, but not the year of the date. This could easily be last or last to last year."

I got Richa's point. But then she added again, "But I think it's worth a try."

"What is worth a try?" I asked.

"We need to get to this place C by tomorrow to see for ourselves." She said.

"What? And how do we plan to do this? Unlike the last time, we are being watched this time! There is no way we're sneaking out this time unnoticed!" I tried to explain to her.

"Don't worry. Who said it would go unnoticed?" she said in her usual calm voice.

"Wow, and you think they will allow us to sneak out? Officially?"

"Yes!" Richa said with the usual sparkle in her eyes, "I have a plan."

CHAPTER TWENTY FOUR

Richa has always had a plan. For this situation too, she had one.

"Okay what's the plan, Richa?" I asked as I held my nervously breath for a few seconds.

Richa sat straight now in an attentive position as she began to narrate her plan:

"Look I will need help from both of you in this thing."

We nodded as she further continued.

"Vishal, remember day before yesterday or so how we sneaked out of the camp for our adventure?"

"Yeah, like I could forget that!" I answered.

"Well, we'll be doing it again. This time, with Kaushal's permission."

"What?" I wasn't sure if heard the right thing. Kaushal would be the last person on earth to grant permission to Richa and me to sneak out of the camp once again. Also, now that they kept a close watch on Richa, it was impossible even to cross the gate without them noticing.

"Yes, we will be sneaking out yet again, with Kaushals' permission." Richa replied calmly.

I still had the question mark on my face as Karan watched with open mouth at Richa.

She continued:

"See, there's one advantage on our side. Kaushal still thinks that Vishal is very faithfully working for them keeping me in darkness. Whereas only we know that you aren't on any one such side and you're here to seek the truth by listening to both of us at your own will. So now, what you will do is, you will go up to Kaushal and tell him that I am asking you to sneak out with me once again. And this time, it's very important. Convince him to let both of us out of here for another day just like we did before and promise him that you will tell him everything that I tell you and where take you to once we escape and return as you have gained my confidence and that could be beneficial to them. Just convince him that you will keep him updated on everything you do with me."

"Sorry, this is a bit confusing." Karan interrupted, "Why will Kaushal grant this?"

"For obvious reason that I am working for him." I replied, "And he will think that now that I have gained Richas' confidence, it will be safe to let me go with her as that might lead them to get to know some more secrets about her through me!"

"Now you are getting it." Richa smiled.

"But what if he sends some of his guys behind you two just in case to keep a watch?" Karan asked. It was a valid question.

Richa took time to answer the question. "See, actually he won't, in the fear of me finding it out and then once I do, I won't take Vishal to the place I was initially going to take him. Kaushal is a smart guy. He won't jeopardize the situation by sending another of his men behind us when he already has Vishal under him." Richa said, "This is just a chance we will have to take."

"Won't that be stupid?"

"No, we're actually betting on Kaushal's intelligence. He won't feel any need to increase the risk by sending spies behind us when he already has his guy Vishal with me." Richa said.

"Okay, so consider I convince I ask Kaushal to let the two us off the camp. I will tell him that you were asking me to sneak out with you once again, and I think this time I might get some good evidence to Kaushal if I were allowed to go. Also I'll promise him that I will be reporting every detail of our outing to him. What happens next?" I asked Richa.

"Next there's nothing like it! We sneak out, without the fear of being caught because Kaushal himself would have allowed us to sneak out thinking I'll share some information or take you to some secrete place, which they'll get eventually through you!" Richa concluded.

"No, I mean we'll sneak out okay, but why are we doing it?"

"To visit this Place C on the map. We will be visiting the first two places and then end our outing on this place C. We can look for some more evidences there; if at all anything is there." Richa answered.

"You think it's worth it?"

"I don't know. See, as I said the map and the dates could be of last year or maybe even older. But there is a tiny possibility that those date could also refer to tomorrow. And we have to cash on it. This is how investigation works, dude. Leave no stone unturned."

"Okay, I understand." I said, "We fool Kaushal into thinking that I'm going with you just because you would be showing me some secret of yours that would help him as an 'evidence' for him against you. But once we're out we'll be visiting the places on the map which has a place marked C with tomorrows date marked in there. We could actually witness something or maybe nothing."

"Yes." Richa said.

"I don't know what to say." I said.

"Just believe in me." Richa placed her hand on mine as she spoke looking at me, "This one last time help me. I have a feeling that this might be one epic outing of ours."

I hoped that too, but in a good positive way epic.

"And what about me?" Karan spoke now, "You said you will need help of both of us, didn't you?"

"Yes, you would be playing the most important role in my plan." Richa answered.

"And what is that?"

"I'll let you know when the right time comes."

"Why not now?"

"My rule book says; reveal your plans only when absolutely necessary and only when the right time comes. But believe me Karan, the success or failure of this plan will finally rest on your shoulder."

CHAPTER TWENTY FIVE

2.30 p.m.
Post lunch

L unch was over by now. Richa and Karan had gone for their usual stroll while I decided it would be a good time to have a word with Kaushal.

I took a deep breath as I stood outside his office. His office door was half-open and he sat there reading something from a file.

"May I come in sir?" I asked.

"Oh boy, come in son, come in." Kaushal greeted me with a smile.

I entered his office, he told me to have a seat and be comfortable.

"So tell me, what you have got. Anything new?" Kaushal asked.

"Not yet, I'm working on it sir." I answered with a smile.

"Would you have tea or coffee?"

"No sir, thank you."

"Okay what brings you here?"

I sat straight before beginning to answer the question. I was nervous; I always get nervous before telling a lie or trying to fake something. I cleared my throat as I began.

"Sir, there's this one favor I want from you."

"Go on."

"Sir, after our earlier talk I have had much success in gaining Richa's confidence. She I guess has by now complete faith in me."

"Good."

"She is now asking for another sneak out from the camp with me. Just like we did the last time. And I need to do this with her. It might just help your organization in getting some more vital clues as she's going to take me to some place where she's going to show me some secret stuff of hers. It seems really important, and I think we should take this chance."

"Let me call the shots boy. I make the decisions here." Kaushal said.

Kaushal thought for a moment.

"You mean I should ignore your sneak out this time and allow you two to do so? So that you get to know where she's going to take you, which in turn will help us gathering the information?" he summed it up.

"Yes, sir."

"How do I trust you in this Vishal?"

"You have to sir; did I not help you in getting her mobile phone? Am I not blindly relying on you for almost every order of yours? Also, did you not tell me to believe in my senses and act accordingly? I think this time the place where she might take me is very important and that we will surely get to know something more about her."

"I understand." Kaushal said as he nodded, I guessed he was falling into the trap.

"Also Sir, even if you don't allow us to sneak out, by some way or the other she will do it on her own alone, and that way we will never be able to find out what she was up to." I added.

Kaushal nodded again.

"So Sir, this one time when we sneak out, just ignore us and let us do whatever she's up to. I will be reporting every single move of hers and collecting any evidence or suspicious observations during the event. If I don't accompany her this time, she will think it is a breach of trust and stop sharing information with me that she's blindly willing to share now." I said.

"Okay, but don't you think it'll be too risky? This time as you say she might actually be up to something dangerous. We can never say." Kaushal said after a thought.

"She trusts me Sir, she'll do nothing to harm me at least. Also now that I will be risking sneaking out with her for the second consecutive time, it will restore even more faith in me, from her side." I answered like a pro.

"No, but I still care for your security." Kaushal answered as he scratched his forehead, "See, just to be on the safe side I will be sending two people from my side behind you. Richa won't even notice that you are being observed. In case of any unfortunate incident these people will rescue you."

This was a boomerang now. This was the last thing Richa and I wanted. People behind us observing us would hamper our entire mission. They would obviously know that Richa and I aren't out for any of her secret locations, but we would be out for the places marked in the map! The places where Kaushal and his team in the workshop might have something to do with! These people observing us would then immediately report this to him and everything would end. I had to think of something. Fast.

"No Sir!" I spoke up, "This I don't think would be a good idea. This Richa seems like a professional, and if she gets any hint that we're being followed, your purpose would fail. She might not take me where she wanted to or share with me whatever she desired to."

"But then what if-."

"Sorry to interrupt you sir" this was the first time I cut Kaushal short from his sentence, I was in control now, "You have to trust me Sir, there's nothing that could go wrong. Just have faith and let me do this for once. I won't disappoint you."

Kaushal then stopped to think once more.

"Okay. I will allow this. But stay safe and get whatever you can in form of information or evidence. Keep your eyes and ears open!" he said.

"Yes Sir" I said as I further informed him that we would be sneaking out tomorrow morning most probably. He okayed the plan and told me that he would talk to the guards and not let them 'catch' us while sneaking out.

I thanked him for his co-operation and began to leave when he called out.

"And listen boy." he said as I turned back to him.

"Yes sir?"

"You remember those ID-cards that were distributed to you people a couple of days ago?"

"Yes"

"Make sure you have them on all the time even while you're out of this camp."

"Yes sir, any specific reason?"

"Yes, they've been installed with a special advanced state of the art GPS tracking systems. We did it to keep a watch on the students once we found out about the transmitter in Richa's locker. We usually give this only to our delivery persons when they travel with cash or any sensitive material to keep track of their movement. But this was the first time we found it essential to use it on our students, for obvious reasons. So even if you both have escaped the camp, you will always be tracked with respect to your current location if not physically by my men."

I went speechless. The whole purpose of Richa's plan seemed to be suddenly defeated.

He continued, "So even if I don't have any of my men to safeguard you, be relaxed as we will always receive a 'live' location feed from your specialized ID cards to our computer."

I didn't know what to say now; I had my foot in my mouth as I said, "Thank you Sir."

"But what if Richa threw it away as soon as we get out of the camp? Or she decides not to carry it with her on our journey? I mean I obviously cannot force her to wear this all the time as that would make her suspicious, isn't it?" I added.

Kaushal smiled, "Let her do whatever she wants with her ID, you keep yours with you. Hide yours in your pocket at least, if not on display. This will keep your position tracked and eventually we'll know where both of you are."

I had an instant feel of my entire convincing Kaushal going down the drain. He had given us the permission, without anyone being on a watch, but with these specialized ID-cards our locations would be tracked. They would know where we're heading. If I did not take my ID card with me, he'll know that I betrayed him and would send a search party, if I carried I-card all along; Kaushal would not sent a search party but would still know of our tour locations! Smart move.

It was all messed up now and I had no clue if Richa had a plan ready for such situations too. I just hoped she had, like always. And if she did, it better be damn good this time.

CHAPTER TWENTY SIX

3.35 p.m.

Merely 20 minutes after I had my chat with Kaushal, I was in the classroom seated with all the students waiting for our post-lunch lecture to start. The two-hour free time as per schedule provided by the workshop was cut down to one and a half hours of free time and the 4.00p.m. lecture was pre-poned to 3.30p.m. I had no time to share my conversation with Kaushal with Richa and Karan. We all waited in our usual Class-4, the classroom to the end of the corridor on the ground floor of the building. We waited for Mr. Sharman Ahuja, our next lecturer.

This was the first time he was conducting a lecture in this schedule of 14 days and I had heard quite a lot about his teaching techniques and presentations from the previous batches and experiences that people had given at the times when I was doing my usual research about the workshop earlier.

He arrived 5 minutes late. He was a man with an average height and fair complexion. The glasses that he wore were professor-like with thread-like-string attached to them going around his neck.

He looked like any other normal person walking casually on the

157

streetwithhishalf-sleeveshirtnottuckedinhistrousersbecausethose were hardly ironed. He entered the classroom with a welcoming smile, gazed the entire room adjusting his glasses, and them spoke, "So, good-afternoon friends!"

Everybody wished him good-afternoon in chorus.

He then rubbed his hands together as he spoke further.

"So friends, how did you find the workshop so far? What all did you learn?"

Yet another lecture that starts with a question, I couldn't resist but observe.

There were mixed responses from the people. Mostly positive. I glanced at my left where Karan and Richa were. Karan smiled at me, while Richa had a curious look in her eyes. I knew what that meant. She wanted to know what had happened between Kaushal and me. Did he grant us the permission to sneak out? Did he fall into the trap? Little did she knew that more than him falling into our trap, it were we who had fallen into his, without him knowing it. I returned an awkward smile to both of them and then looked in the front, at Mr. Ahuja.

"Something's missing here." He said looking around.

There was a murmur around. He glanced at the students, and then the four classroom walls. Then with a brisk movement of his head and dramatically raising his tone to a certain level he said, "This just isn't my way of teaching you guys. Let's get out of here."

There was murmuring yet again, this time louder. Ahuja saw the confusion and then smiled as he stated further, "Education or knowledge cannot be gained in a closed environment. It should always be in an open one. How can you open your mind to new ideas when your body is trapped in a closed place?"

Half of what he said didn't make much sense to me. I was busy thinking what Richa would say when I told her about my conversation with Kaushal. Little did she know that those specialized ID cards we had for last 2 days have been giving out our location from minute to minute to some temporarily setup control room in this building. Every move ours was being monitored and it was impossible to visit the restricted places, rather we would be caught long before we even reached there.

Suddenly, I gave a break to my stream of thoughts as I saw the students getting up from their seats. I wondered what had I missed. Then I understood that it was Mr. Ahujas' idea to have the lecture outside the classroom, in the lawn. He wanted to conduct it in an 'open environment' rather than in a classroom. This was the very first time any session, other than the Yoga, was to be conducted the lawn.

We all walked to the corridor making our way to the lawn area, when Richa caught up with me as she asked, "So what happened? Did he agree?"

"Yeah, kind of." I said as I struggled to keep the pace with the moving students.

"You mean?"

"It's quite complicated, we have the permission but—."

"Yay! He granted the permission no? Then that's it. Leave the rest to me." She never gave me any chance to complete my sentence. This time it was essential for her to let me do so. But I decided to let her know about it later as I didn't want a debate right now, when a class was in progress.

Within a couple of minutes about all of us comprising of 38-40 students stood in the lawn area as Ahuja stood there right in front of us, welcoming us to his class with a bright smile.

"So I hereby welcome you all to my class, where the nature is the teacher and I'm the interpreter." He said with his arms wide open.

Everyone clapped. The students were very pleased by this different approach of Ahuja to teaching. They now had high expectations from him. We all now sat with our legs crossed on the lawn, without any mat or piece of cloth laid on it. Richa sat beside me and Karan in front.

"Today this lecture might just make you look at our rituals, customs and traditions from a different angle altogether. This is where Science will meet religion, customs and rituals. This, my friends, is like the *Circus* of believers and non-believers!" He said, "But before beginning I would like to show you something, and for that I need a few minutes. I'll be right back." He said as he kept us seated and left somewhere inside the building.

Students began talking amongst themselves just as school children do when the teacher leaves the classroom for a minute or two.

"So we're going then?" Karan asked as he turned back instantly after Ahuja left.

"No, we are going." Richa said, "We as in, Vishal and me."

"But you said I had a very important role to play in your sneak out! Didn't you!" Karan fought back.

"Yes, and you are." Richa told him, "Listen to my plan first."

Just as always, I wasn't even given a fair chance to have my say, yet.

"See, about tomorrow early morning Vishal and I would be leaving the camp, let's say at about 5 a.m. That would be approximately about an hour before the Yoga session." Richa began to tell her plan for the next day, "We will then make it to the first two places marked in the map to explore there and then about in the afternoon visit the place that has tomorrow's date marked on it. Place C"

Karan was listening with a keen ear. He was still trying to figure out where his role was in this.

"This is when Karan comes into play." Richa finally said, "I will be giving you a number before we escape. All you have to do is manage an escape for yourself after the lunch hours while the usual strolling in the lawn. And—."

"In broad daylight!?" Karan was alarmed. Later he realized he had almost actually yelled out the question and then contained his excitement level.

"Yes." Richa said in her usual calm tone, "How you escape is up to you and you will have to do it without anyone knowing it. I trust you on this and believe that you will do it. I'm relying on you for this."

Karan nodded half-heartedly. Richa continued:

"Once you are out of the camp, all you have to do is call a number that I will be giving to you before we leave from here using any safe roadside P.C.O booth to the head office of our News Agency. Get in touch with Mr. Javed Khan and ask them to reach the location where we would be waiting by then."

"You mean Place C as given in the map?" Karan asked.

"Yes" Richa said, "All of this will end there. If any event is to happen there by tomorrow, we will witness it, all at once. My agency people will conduct a sting or cover it 'live'. This will be one hell of an expose operation."

"What if we don't find anything?" I asked.

"You know, in the world of investigations things do mess up at 'n' number of times, it's only about how you handle them at that point. Whenever our agency gets any input from any of our sources, 80% of time we return empty handed, they're mostly hoax. So we have to be prepared for nothings as well as everything. In that case, if nothing happens as such, we'll return to the camp as we did earlier and make up some story by then." Richa answered.

"Don't you think you're taking this too easy?"

"No, this is the only way the operation could be carried out now. We have no other choice."

"Why don't you make a call from your cell phone from here itself to your agency and ask them to raid the locations without us leaving the camp and risking it?" I asked.

"Good question." Richa smiled, "But there are two issues. One of them is that you had earlier handed over my cell-phone to the workshop authorities, and I don't want to risk anything by making any call from that cell-phone now. My phone could be doctored with anything by now."

It was valid point.

"And number two is that without knowing for sure that there's at least something over there, we cannot involve our agency. There's so much at stake. These *A Way Around* people could drag our agency into various lawsuits and demand a ban on it in case we don't find anything in there. Anything stupid and these organization people will kill my agency by filing a defamation case in the court! In case we, as in just the two of us, are caught, the maximum any court could do is dismiss us as just another 'adventurous kids' or give some negligible punishment, or detention."

"What?" I wasn't even sure if she was saying all of this, she was calmly saying about our jurisdiction by the court as if it didn't matter much and was a game show. I felt like that hen who was being fed well just so that she could be well cooked later.

"That is the worst case scenario Vishal! Chill please." she assured me.

"But it is a scenario right?" I protested.

She ignored my question.

"But why does Karan have to call your agency? That too after half of the day is over? Why cannot we call them from outside once we've escaped from here?" I asked further.

"Because right things are to be done at the right time. Firstly I'm asking him to call the agency post lunch after his escape from here because about that time we will be at the Place C and that is the time they should be there. If we alert them earlier they might rush into the matter in order to get the first hand report and I do not want to jeopardize anything. Also, I'm asking him rather than us to make the call for the simple reason that we cannot say if we will be in a position to make the call at the crucial moment. Anything could go wrong in the due course of our trail. If there are guards there and they find us, they might capture us; we might not be in position to get near a phone at that time, who knows? Considering all of this, it's safe that Karan makes the call safely once he's out so that no matter what, my agency people are dispatched to the place we would be by then."

"What if Karan doesn't manage to sneak out?"

"Well, he has to. There are always ifs and buts in every operation and a number of things could go wrong. But we do have to rely on certain things and believe that they will go according to the plan. No plan is 100% fool proof, but it should be 100% well thought out." She replied.

I was dumbstruck. And so was Karan. It was all scary as hell. It seemed that now our lives were at stake. The documentary mission suddenly didn't matter to me at all. It all had come down to our lives!

"So guys are you with me?"

We kept quiet. She looked at both of us and raised her eyebrows.

"Yes." Karan and I said hesitating a bit.

This I thought was the time wherein I could tell Richa about our specialized ID-cards that apparently had the location transmitter and ask her about what plan she had for it.

"Richa, all of this is okay. But there's one major obstacle in our mission."

"And what is that?" she asked.

I looked down at my ID-card and picked an end of it as it hung by my neck, "This –."

Before even I went further explaining its purpose, Ahuja returned with a plastic bag in his hand.

"Did you miss me, friends!" he said smiling back at his students.

The discussion and the murmurs within the students stopped as all of them turned towards him.

The three of us too, stopped our discussion as we turned towards him. Yet again, I didn't manage to tell her about the most critical thing that would surely lead to the failure of our mission to point C. The moment we visited the points A and B we would be tracked down and held captive before we reached the point C. Also even if I decided to give the ID a skip or damage the card, it would send a signal that I was on Richa's side now and they would again track us down using man power and bring us to justice by all means. For the first time I felt Richa's plan led to a dead end. For the first time I felt, everything wasn't actually all right, even though I had Richa on my side.

CHAPTER TWENTY SEVEN

"So friends, there are no points for guessing here, because I think you know what this is." Ahuja said as he pulled out an *Amla* fruit from the carry bag that he had just got and displayed it in his hand.

A couple of people answered *"Amla!"*

"Yes." Ahuja said, "This is *Amla* or known as *Phyllanthus Embilca* in the botanical world." There were a few quips when Ahuja said the botanical name of the fruit. He noticed it, waited for a second and then went on.

"Now the plant and this fruit, plays a very important role in terms of medicines. It is an important ingredient in many *ayurvedic* medicines and tonics. One *Amla* can provide you with the same amount of Vitamin C that two oranges would. Modern research has proved that *Amla* is an effective food supplement during the treatment of insulin dependent Diabetes as found in a study conducted in Coimbatore."

Even though the students loved the unusual share of information on a random topic they were getting at Ahuja's class, no one was sure where exactly he was heading.

"Also, do you know what these are?" He further asked as he

drew out some leaves from the bag.

Students tried to guess one after the other. He did not say which of them had answered correctly.

He just smiled at every answer.

"This, my friends is *Azadirachta Indica*, or *Neem* as we commonly call it." He explained, "This has been used in the Indian sub–continent far about 4500 years! Its medicinal values have a good use in blood purification, arthritis and removal of internal and external parasites. It's also used as an insect repellent in villages. This is an important ingredient in *ayurvedic* creams and gels which can be used to treat problems like dry skin, wrinkles, dandruff, skin ulcers etc. Modern research has proven that a juice of tender *neem* leaves and a tea-spoon of honey can be consumed to flush out toxins in the liver and other disorders. *Neem* is known to have medicinal values. Being bitter, it works wonders in diseases like diabetes. One table spoon of *neem* leaves juice taken early morning also controls diabetes."

I looked at Richa, and she looked back at me. We were as puzzled as were the other students.

"So this just one of the few herbal or medicinal plants that I wanted to introduce to you before I begin with the topic for today. There are so many other plants and herbs that you come across in your day to day life that have some magical medicinal values. Tamarind, *Tulsi*, *Aloe Vera* and many others!" Ahuja said excitedly.

The moment Ahuja stopped speaking, there was clapping. There was nothing much that Ahuja had done till now other than sharing information on the medicinal plants with us, but the sheer excitement he had in doing so and the energy with which he threw that information at us, made us all applaud. In the end, it was all about presentation.

"So why do you think I've been telling you all this? This isn't a botany class is it?" He asked smiling at us.

We didn't have the answer.

"Okay, tell me, what you think. Modern day diseases like diabetes, backache, skin problems, obesity, hypertension etc. are so common now. Were they common about a century back? They were actually, there but were very rare and treatable I tell you."

This very question of Ahuja made me think this was just another *technology-is-bad-and-made-us-more-prone-to-diseases* kind of lecture.

"Sir, now you'll blame it on technology and globalization." some girl from the third row from the front said as if she had just read my mind.

Ahuja smiled, "That's not where I'm heading to."

He kept the plastic bag aside as he began walking to and fro.

"You remember the age old customs and traditions that we were always told to follow and we still do, according to our own respective religions?" He said, "You think they were created with an aim or just like that?"

There was confusion. People didn't quite get the question that was shot at them. Ahuja like a pro sensed the situation and re-framed his question, "I mean take the *Hindu* religion for instance. These consisted of the *Brahmins* who were the scholars of that time and liberated the society on what was to be done on certain events. They recited *shlokas* and conducted *pujaas*, that is religious prayers, during festivals or auspicious occasions at people's homes, gave them advice on astrology, and told them what was essential for them. You think all that happened for a reason?"

I couldn't stay quiet for long now, I raised my hand to get an answer to my query, "Sir, basically during the times that you're talking about, people did have plenty of time to do stuff. There were fewer things to do and more time with people to deal with it. So according to me, such rituals and traditions along with the festivals every season was man's own way to keep himself occupied and socialized."

"Hmm. Good answer, but a very generic one, if I may say."

Ahuja said as he began to explain further, "You see, the plants that I discussed earlier in my lecture, every single plant with a medicinal quality is linked to some ritual or the other in our religion. For instance, the *Amla* leaves are used in the month of *marga-shirsha* that is November/December to worship Goddess Laxmi. The *Neem* leaves are used in many of the rituals and offerings in the Hindu culture. The *tulsi*, the coconut. Everything. Almost every possible rare or common medicinal or valuable herb or plant is in some way or the other is a part of the culture. Why only these plants are part of all these auspicious rituals? Why not other flowers and plants which are available anywhere in bulk?"

'So?' I thought. I still wasn't getting his point.

"So what I mean to say is, it was the *pujaaris* of that time who decided to come up with such ingredients in their rituals right? I mean the Gods did not obviously descend from the skies to tell us the recipe for religious prayers! And why were these occasional rituals and festivals with necessity of such apparatus made necessary by the *pujaaris*? For the simple reason that they wanted every person to be surrounded in some way or the other by these natural medicines! When you are in need of certain elements from time to time you do make sure that you are in touch with time more often. Right?"

"Isn't that a long shot Sir?" the girl from the front row asked, "I mean those scholars or *pujaaris* could easily have told the people about the importance of these plants and told them to preserve them than making up these rituals in the name of God?"

"They certainly could have." Ahuja answered, "But then people wouldn't have cared much. We are a very religious country. When asked to fast for a day just for nothing we cannot control our appetite. But when it's done in the name of God, we can go through the entire day without even water!"

Now slowly I was getting his point. This lecture was turning from just another lecture at the workshop to a very profound one.

"Consider the case of solar eclipses." Ahuja said further, "Scientists say that they aren't to be looked at with your naked eyes. If the illiterate people of the past were told that the eclipse would harm their eyes, only a few would pay any heed to such slogans. What scholars chose then was to make up a mythological story that kept people away from even getting out of their houses to watch it."

He was now referring to the Chinese story that was told to kids since the ancient times. According to the myth (which was later transformed to a superstition) the demons ate up the Sun that caused the darkness on Earth rather than the Moon's shadow doing the trick.

"There are so many things in our mythology that coincided with scientific facts. Both say the same thing, only the reasoning is different. Science gives facts, geographical evidences, laws of physics and equations. Whereas mythology and religions give the cause of the gods and demons. People believe and follow religion more than they even understand Science."

The lecture seemed even more interesting as he went on giving us insights into famous mythological stories and beliefs and how they coincided with science at some point.

"Take simpler things for instance. It's said that people shouldn't sleep under any tree at night as the devils and zombies hang upside down on certain types of trees. Modern science may say the same. Only the reason is that trees exhale carbon-dioxide in the night so we might not get enough pure oxygen as we would have got in the day time under the same tree! Now these facts couldn't be explained to the layman of those times and hence the devil story that made sense to him worked wonders!"

"Don't you take this as a spread of superstitions? In the name of God, why would the scholars spread myths and make up stories?" Mr. Khurana, the army uncle asked.

"I get your point, but you see people weren't so open minded back then. Or even now, only the city people and the educated class in India are open minded. There's so much of illiteracy and lack of knowledge in so many parts of our own country. You talk of the internet and there are villages that still do not have electricity!" Ahuja explained, "There was no other option to spread awareness than to attach it to a ritual, that is, their religion and their Gods! You see, we burn and kill in the name of God! Did the scholars of that time have any other option?"

I had never looked back at my religion in a way I had today. This lecture was changing my point of view to look at everything related to my own religion and culture.

This surely proved that we had scholars and experts or 'scientists' as we call them today in the past too. Only their way of educating the masses was different. They explained people simple dos and don'ts in a language that every layman could understand. From the king in his palace to the beggar on the street, everyone understood the language of God, the language of religion. It was like a virtual bridge that connected the scholar to a commoner.

Everything suddenly made sense.

The lecture continued for 45 minutes more which again, due to Einstein's theory of relativity, seemed to me like it had lasted only for like 10 minutes.

"In the end, let's talk about the end." Ahuja said, "You know how the end of the world has been depicted in the *Vedas*?"

No one raised the hands. Most of them hadn't read the *Vedas* and the rest didn't know what they even were. The *Vedas* are nothing but religious scripts written by ancient scholars that contained knowledge on almost everything in religion. It was like the encyclopedia of the *Hindu* religion.

"The *Vedas,* according to my grandmother apparently say that the world ends when the Sun opens its 12 eyes, seeming 12 times the present size and it will rain so heavily that one drop of the rain will be the size of an elephant in which eventually the whole world will drown. Now I don't know how much of this is actually true, but my grandmother had these stories to tell from ancient literature as it was passed on to her by the previous generations. Certainly she hadn't gained this knowledge from *Britannica* or *World Book Encyclopedia*, did she?"

I wasn't really sure how much of that was actually true. But then I hadn't read the *Vedas*, nor had my grandmother told me any such story.

Ahuja stopped for his audience to get the fact digested then he continued,

"Whereas the NASA claims that the Sun will explode in such a way that it will release huge amounts of energy. It will appear 12 times its volume that would cause all the oceans and sea water to evaporate all at once! This will eventually lead to heavy rainfalls everywhere leading into a massive destruction!"

He didn't say anything further. The students got his point. What the NASA claimed would happen, after doing years of research, was already known to the *Vedas* thousands of years back! Same story, different language.

Ahuja was about to end his lecture on this note. Just then students applauded continuously for about two minutes and urged him to share something more on the same topic. On popular demand, Ahuja extended his lecture for fifteen more minutes and then thanked everyone for the overwhelming response as he left.

Even after he left, people didn't get up and stayed seated for the next couple of minutes. They were shaken. Some were shaken due to the sudden burst of some incredible knowledge they just had, some were shaken off their belief system. Slowly everyone got up.

"Wasn't that one amazing lecture!?" I asked as we walked to the classroom.

Karan agreed as he gave me a high-five.

"So tell me, what you were saying." Richa asked.

"About the lecture?"

"No, about the ID card. You were going to say something

about it when Ahuja entered and began his lecture."

The lecture had me completely forget for sometime about the massive mission we had at hand the next morning and the obstacle we had in front of us due to the specialized ID cards, which were nothing but a location transmitter, which made us nothing but a digital dot on some screen of a computer somewhere in this building.

"Ahh" I said, "See, your plan is fool-proof and all I understand. I understand the roles we are to play and that Karan will be playing. But there's a major hitch in it. These ID cards won't let us do what we want up to."

"What do you mean?" Richa asked.

I lowered my voice as I now spoke in whispers to Richa, "I mean these are transmitting our current locations to Kaushal 24X7 and once they see our digital dots on their computer map-screen tomorrow heading towards their locations, I don't think they'll spare us! How are we going to do it?"

"Just damage the ID cards!" Karan said

"No!" Richa said instantly, "That would be like inviting them and challenging them that we are against your organization! We will have to do it without damaging the ID cards, and rather keeping them with us all the time. This will keep them relaxed and once they're able to know our each and every move because of this, they won't try something drastic and just observe."

"But won't it be stupid? I mean how will they just sit and watch on their computers when they will be able to see us walking into those locations that seemingly are important to them!"

"They will, don't worry" Richa said with a smile, "I have a plan for that too."

Yet again, Richa had proved me wrong.

She still had a plan.

CHAPTER TWENTY EIGHT

Day 8
4.45 a.m.

I was dreaming. It had something to do with my documentary. I dreamt that it had been received well everywhere and I was at the Discovery Channel's Prize Distribution ceremony. There was a huge nicely decorated hall with ribbons and stuff, full of people. A stage brightly lit up and with some couple of men in suits.

And then they announce my name "Vishal Rajguru!" There was clapping. A thunderous one.

As I went ahead to receive my prize, which was a trophy and a certificate, I was then handed over the mike to say a word or two about my feeling. The guy handing over the mike to me said, "Hey.. Get up *dumbo*! We got to go!"

I was puzzled and soon that guy started shaking me.

"Get up!" He said now in a female voice as I realized the shake was getting stronger.

Within half a minute I was out of my dream. Now wide awake.

I got up and saw Richa standing beside my bed shaking me.

My dream was over.

I glanced at the watch placed at the table. 4:45a.m, it said.

Richa had come to wake me up for our new mission. Karan was awake too. He sat on his bed right opposite to mine.

"Hurry up; we've to leave before the dawn breaks." Richa said.

I got up to freshen up myself.

About 15 minutes later, I was back in the room.

"So? Ready?" Richa asked as she punched me on my arm playfully.

"Yes, I guess." I said as I reached out to my ID-card that hung on the hook. I took it and placed it in my trouser pocket.

The ID-card could have been avoided, but then that would not go well with Kaushal and he would instantly understand that I cheated him by lying to him. So in order to have the trust restored, he had to know where we were going.

"This ID-card thing is going to ruin our mission." I said to Richa.

"No it won't." She replied instantly.

"Did I not tell you that this piece of device has an inbuilt location transmitter? It's like a mini-GPS for God's sake!"

"Yes I know. We're going to use his weapon against him."

"What do you mean?"

"We will use this to mis-lead him, rather than lead to us. Karan will be the only person knowing about our locations. This ID-card of Kaushal isn't going to help him."

"We cannot destroy it! He will –."

"We won't. Just wait, and watch."

Karan then got up from his bed as he held us both with both of his hands.

"Good luck both of you." He said.

Richa thanked him as we all did a group hug.

"You know what you're supposed to do right?" Richa asked.

"Yes. After lunch I'll make my way outside the camp without

anyone knowing. And call on the number you've given me, and get those people from your agency to Place C as per the map." Karan briefed.

While I was freshening up, Richa had written down her News Agency's number and an alternate number on a chit of paper and given it to Karan. She had asked him to memorize it and destroy the chit later.

"Good. And in case Kaushal asks you anything about us? Obviously he won't because he already knows we would go missing, only the thing he doesn't in know the purpose behind it." Richa said smiling.

"I will say I have no idea. Just like I did not have any the first time you people escaped."

"Good." Richa said, "But make sure you carefully sneak out post-lunch and no one knows about it. Or there's a high risk of you being followed or even captured, because our sneak out is authorized, not yours! Our entire success rests on your shoulders"

"Don't pressurize him and all.." I interrupted, "I know he'll do okay. He's not a kid!"

"Okay now go you both! Its 5a.m." Karan said checking his watch.

Richa and I wished luck to Karan as we walked out through the corridors to the locker.

Richa and I opened our respective lockers. She took her belongings with her and so did I.

Wallet, cell-phone, and the box. The one that she had given me with all the combination lock on it.

"What about this?" I asked her showing her the secret box.

"Take that with you. You just might need it, if something goes wrong."

"What?"

"Just in case. Don't worry; you might never even need it."

"But I still don't know the password!!"

"Well, believe me, you do." Richa said with a grin.

I hated it when she talked in code.

"No, you didn't tell me."

"No I didn't, but you know. It's just that you haven't realized it yet."

"Damn! What is wrong with you Richa! Can you at least tell me what is it that will contain all the answers in this box?"

"A phone number" Richa said.

"A phone what? Insane! What phone number?"

"Mine" she joked, "In case you wanted to ask me out later after our today's date."

"Oh, God Richa you're unbelievable!" I was losing my temper, "All you wrote on that little strip of paper is a phone number? And concealed it in this box to which I don't even know the password!? Are you nuts?" I was losing my temper.

"You see, the moment I see the need to tell you the password to this box, I will do it. And that will be the time when I wouldn't be of any help to you. That's when you call the number. He will help you in any possible way! He can save you from any.. believe me, any problem. Help you with any issues of yours. Trust me."

"Who he? God?"

"Maybe!" Richa giggled.

"Oh I can't believe I'm doing this with you"

"Shhh.. now pocket it and let's get out of here!"

I stuffed my two trouser pockets with my wallet, a chain of mine, my cell-phone and the little box Richa had given me.

We then made it through the moon-lit lawn. We looked out for a safe portion of the compound where we weren't visible to the two watchmen taking their usual rounds, and climbed past over it.

With a thud Richa landed on the other side of the compound first, followed by me.

My ID card fell out of my pocket due to the jerk. I picked it up and tugged it inside again.

"I still have no clue how you manage to fool Kaushal with

this thing constantly giving out our locations to him."

"Stop and get over it now. And move!" Richa said as we finally made our way out of the camp and started walking further.

I had no idea what Richa meant or how she was going to mis-lead Kaushal using his own weapon. But now that she had said it, I had faith in her. I guess this is what we called blind faith. As rightly said, it's like taking a step even when we don't see a staircase.

CHAPTER TWENTY NINE

2.45 p.m.
Inside the Camp,
Post lunch time

About roughly 9 hours after our miraculous escape, it was finally the afternoon time. At the camp, Karan was nervous. It was time. It was time for him to sneak out from the camp. For last 15minutes Karan had been taking rounds of the lawn. Just like others did after their lunch. Everyone chatted with each other, discussed about the lectures or some other topics with their newly made friends at the camp. Karan was walking all alone. His mind was cluttered with thoughts, mostly contained 'ifs and buts' to which he feared he did not have any answers.

He looked at everyone else in the lawn. They were in their own little worlds. He looked at the guards; they were on their usual to and fro rounds. Karan now made his way to the back side of the lawn, where usually no student went. He planned to get out by climbing over the small exit behind the lawn. His legs had begun to tremble as he made his way towards the gate.

He reached out his pocket and checked if he had taken his belongings with him. Mainly, the money and the chit of paper on which Richa had given the number of her agency. As told by Richa he had to memorize the number and destroy the chit rather than carrying it with him.

"It would be too risky in case you are caught." She had told him.

But in all the nervousness and tension of making out of the camp safely, Karan had not memorized the number and he feared he would forget it. He placed the chit back into his pocket and walked further.

He now held the gate bars with both his hands. There was a lock on the gate. The exit-gate at the back-side of the building always had a lock on it, unlike the front gate which was wide open for anyone to enter or leave. Students where allowed out only for two hours after lunch. Karan would have got out of that gate straight away, and did what Richa had told him to do once he was out, but there was a risk. The guards frisked every student before leaving the camp and also when they returned. Karan had his phone, money and the chit given by Richa with him. According to the camp rules, possession money or any of the digital distraction was prohibited for 14 days. He would be caught and taken into interrogation immediately.

Karan now took a deep breath as he placed his right leg on one of the horizontal gate bars. He looked right, and then left and with a jerk pushed himself up. Then climbed over the gate finally making way to the other side of the compound. After less than a minute he landed on the ground.

As he landed down he slipped, stumbled and fell on his face. He soon regained his posture and turned away to walk further when he heard a voice behind him, it was familiar,

"Boy, are you hurt?"

Karan saw to his left and about two-three feet away next to the compound Kaushal stood there smiling at him. Karan did not know what to do.

"So? Where were you planning to escape? To join your

friends?" Kaushal said as he walked up to Karan with a hint of anger in his eyes and further a bully like tone, "I always knew there was something fishy going on the moment that friend of yours suddenly and smoothly started following our orders. Escaping with that chick and all to help us? Bullshit that was, isn't it! We'll I'm sorry to break it to you, but it seems that this won't end well, especially if you're friend is on the wrong side."

CHAPTER THIRTY

About 8 hours ago,
Just after Vishal & Richa's escape,
Early morning,

"Stop playing with that I-Card!" Richa for once scolded me as she saw me nervously fidgeting with it.

"What! I'm nervous!" I said.

"Just stay calm and walk!" She ordered.

It was about 20 minutes after we had sneaked out of the camp as per our plan. Richa had the map in her hand. I was busy looking around if anyone followed us. It was still darkish outside. The sun would be up in about next fifteen minutes or so.

For the next five minutes no one spoke. And then Richa spoke.

"Tea or coffee?" she asked.

"What?"

"Tea or Coffee?"

"How can you-."

"TEA or COFFEE?"

"Tea"

"Hmm.. keep walking."

I gave her a weird look which she ignored. After a minute walk she took me to a corner tea shop at a road junction.

Early morning walkers, newspaper-*wallas*, quite a few *richshaw-wallas* were kind of having their daily re-union there at the tea stall this early morning. Richa, was the only female customer.

"You'll have anything else?" she asked me.

I didn't know what to say, "Yes, *Biryani* please."

She made a crooked face and tapped me on my head.

"Good PJ, wrong timing." She said as she turned to the tea stall owner, "*Bhaiiya, 2 chaai aur ek Cream-Roll dena please*"

"I don't want.. –." I began to object.

"It's for me, didn't you hear? ONE cream-roll, and that's for me."

I kept quite. In about a minute a boy working at the tea stall gave us our two teas and a cream-roll.

We drank it in silence. If it was for any other day, I would have treasured this moment. But not today, we had too much of a task at hand to enjoy anything in the world.

"Richa, seriously, what's wrong with you? Why are you behaving like this with me?" I asked.

"What is wrong with you, Vishal? It seems that you don't trust me enough. Whatever you're doing to help me seems that you're doing it reluctantly. Do you really even want to find out the truth?" Richa asked as she sipped her tea.

"Of course I do! But your methods are very much questionable. Without much proof, evidence you set out on a mission like this that could well jeopardize our existence! Why do we have to do everything? Is it really worth it?"

"Of course it is Vishal. You talk of proof and evidence, but isn't that what we are actually out looking for? Don't you have any sense of giving some service towards society? Are you so selfish Vishal?"

"Where does society come into this now? I'm just saying that

I was not prepared for all this when I enrolled for the camp!"

"We're never ready for anything in life buddy. God throws in such surprises and opportunities to lucky ones. Don't you want to try something else than live a routine life? Consider if we succeed in this mammoth task, just think what wonders it could do to us!"

"That's a lot of ifs and buts, Richa."

"So you're Mr. Half-Glass-Empty?"

I kept mum. She always did that. One question and you question yourself. As if she knew more about me than me. Now whatever was done was done. I was out of the camp with her, to seek 'truth', 'evidence' and whatever it was. There was no turning back.

"Anyways, let's hurry there, we got to finish place A & B before we head to place C." I reminded Richa as she was merrily enjoying her tea-breakfast.

"Nah, we're heading to Place C. Directly." she answered without looking up.

"Why the sudden change of plan?" I asked.

"No sudden. We always were going to head to place C."

"But you said in the morning, and yesterday that we would be visiting all three places!"

"Yes, Karan was there. Never reveal your entire plan in front of the third-party."

"Third party? It was Karan for god's sake!"

"I know. But rules are rules."

"And what would you get by hiding the actual plan from Karan?"

"See, it's like a safety measure. In case Karan is caught and forced to blurt out the truth. This is all he'll know that we would be visiting all three places. For him, that's the truth. So even if a trap is laid by Kaushal, he'll divert his attention to the first two places and then to the third place. Reduces the risk you see. Even if he sends a search party for us, it'll be divided in the three mentioned places."

This was sheer brilliance. All I wanted to do was touch her feet in front of the tea stall vendor and all the other customers there, as clearly, this girl had a brain that comprised of intelligence more than all the intelligence of the people present there, including mine.

"Okay, but don't you think it would be worth visiting place A and B too?" I asked as we finished with our morning tea, made payment to the vendor and walked further.

"No." Richa said, "You know, Place A and B are past. Whatever was to be done there by these people has already been done there on the given two dates that have already passed away. It's no use going there now. Also, when any illegal activity is carried out somewhere, the place is obviously spring-cleaned later. Kaushal is a smart man. He'll always erase the evidences and come clean once crime is done. He'll never leave a crime scene without washing out the stains of his crimes. What we are interested now is what will happen today, at the third place. And we have only one chance. Now."

I got her point. We walked further.

Soon we came towards a flyover.

"Come." she asked me to follow her.

Soon we were on the flyover. The sun had risen by then. It looked wonderful. But the scenic beauty was certainly not why she had got me here. At right in the middle of the flyover she stopped and leaned towards the side of the flyover. I looked down. There were heavy vehicles and very few four wheelers running down the bridge.

"What?" I asked.

"Let me solve one of your problems first." Richa grinned.

"By what? Pushing me down the bridge?" I gulped.

"No *Dumbo*! Hand that I-Card to me."

"No way! You cannot destroy it!" I fought back.

"I AM NOT." she stared in my eyes.

I gave up and handed the I-card to her.

She took it in her hand, and waited. Initially I couldn't understand what she was trying to do, but then I got it. She waited for an open roof cargo truck to be spotted from the bridge. She held the I-card now loosely by its neck string. With perfect timing as the truck was just about to pass below the bridge, she let it go. The I-Card landed on the truck cargo box, a few feet below the bridge.

She then looked at me and smiled.

"See, there goes your worry." She then dusted her hands as we began to walk away again.

She did it again. Technically, she did not destroy the I-card and it was still giving out location signals to Kaushal. But now it was gone with the truck somewhere in the city. Kaushal would be a fool to follow the path now. Whatever directions Kaushal got now via the I-card, were wrong.

This was Richa's best plan yet, I guess I should've thought of it. But I was too nervous to think of anything sane today.

Her plan was just like her, simple and brilliant.

CHAPTER THIRTY ONE

Present time,
3.15 p.m.
At the Camp

Karan now stood in Kaushal's office. With his head bowed and eyes glued to the floor. The piece of paper that Richa had given him with the phone number of her agency was swallowed by him on the way to the office soon after the time he was caught in the lawn. Kaushal had not noticed it. But now there was a problem, he had not memorized the number. He did not know where to call now, that is, if he ever got a chance. But that in a way did not even matter right now. All that mattered now was what Kaushal's next step would be. What would he do with Karan.

Kaushal sat in his chair staring at Karan waiting for Karan to speak up.

"So tell me! What's going on here?" Kaushal raised his tone. Karan did not speak a word.

"So Vishal fooled us! I trusted him, granted him the permission to sneak out of the camp with that girl thinking he would help us, but that idiot, fell for the girl's hoax and cheated us! Traitor!" Kaushal was losing his temper now.

"Sir, I have no idea what you are referring to. I myself am looking for both Vishal as well as Richa." Karan lied according to the plan.

"Okay Karan, you have to understand one thing. This isn't going to work with me. Cough up the truth. Tell me where these people are. I know you know." Kaushal spoke with a stern voice.

Karan now understood the game was over. For him at least, it seemed to be over. Kaushal knew what Vishal, Richa and Karan himself were working against him.

"Sir, I can't tell you anything. Also, I don't see any reason for you to be afraid if your organization isn't guilty." Karan finally gathered the courage to say, as he added further, "Also, you are tracking them with the ID-card that is with Vishal, aren't you?"

Kaushal ignored the question as he finally walked up to Karan and placed both his hands on his shoulders as he shook his head in dismay, then said, "Listen Karan, you have to understand a few things over here. None of you is really sure if the girl, Richa is faking it or not. You have no clue if the side that you are supporting is even guilty or not. Did you people find anything conclusive against us yet? No."

"We are working on it." Karan replied boldly.

"You don't understand Karan! I cannot explain everything to you right now, but you people are going to get into a hell of a lot of trouble." Kaushal said.

"Are you threatening me Sir?"

"No. I'm warning you. For your own good, more than mine."

Kaushal then went back to his seat and pressed the buzzer on his table. About in less than a minute two huge security guards marched in to his office.

"Frisk him." Kaushal ordered.

Karan was searched from top to bottom. They found all that he had carried with him during the escape, except the chit that he had swallowed. Karan thanked himself for that.

"So boy, you were pretty well equipped to run away forever

it seems!" Kaushal send looking at the money and iPod that he had with him.

Karan did not reply. With an instant gush the security guard held each of Karans' arms and started acting rough and squeezing his arms.

"No! Don't hurt him!" Kaushal ordered instantly.

Kaushal closed his eyes for a minute and then making himself calm and toning down his voice a level he further spoke, "Listen boy, I have no idea what magic that girl has played on you and your friend. But whatever I'm about to show you, should at least open your eyes wide open. Think in a neutral way once for God's sake! Open your mind and watch without any presumptions. You have to know that you are on the wrong side!"

Karan stayed quiet. The security guards had loosened their grip on him now, but stood close enough to make him nervous. One slap from them could easily make him unconscious and another one could possibly even see the end of him.

Kaushal then opened the drawer of his desk and shuffled a few papers until he found what he was looking for. A blue colored file. He took it into his hands and placed it on the table.

"Sit boy." he asked Karan to be seated in front of him. Karan obeyed.

"This is an extremely confidential data that we are sharing with you. You are making me do this due to your adamant behavior and non-cooperation with us. We could easily have detained and handed you over to the police and the government as soon as we thought you were up to something fishy, but we did not."

"Why didn't you then?"

"Because we are not bad guys! We know that you and your friend Vishal have nothing to do with Richa and whatever she is up to. It's just that you two have been brainwashed by her and used by her against us."

Kaushal then flipped some pages from the file he had opened

and then turned it towards Karan to show him.

"Here, have a look." Kaushal said as he pointed to a document.

Karan pulled the file near to him as he saw. It was an admission form. On the right hand corner of the form there was Richa's photo with the authorized stamp of a college from Bhopal.

"This shows that she's a mechanical engineer student, currently studying at Bhopal." Kaushal said, "Now flip the page."

Karan obeyed again. He flipped a page more and there was another form. Richa again, of the same year.

"Now what is she doing here? Look at the form, admission form for Delhi University, doing Commerce first year. This one is an authentic and stamped by the college stamp too." Kaushal pointed.

Karan observed both the forms. They weren't a Xerox copy or printouts, Kaushal had indeed managed to acquire actual forms of hers filled for the current year.

"But—." Karan was interrupted before he said anything.

"Wait, there's more." Kaushal said as he asked Karan to look more into the file.

There were one more of those, which was a certificate. It was given by an NGO from Hyderabad to Richa for working with them as an intern for one whole year. The year was the current year. Same as the one mentioned in her Engineering as well as Commerce from Bhopal and Delhi respectively.

"And this girl told you that she works as in intern journalist didn't she? This data has been collected by our private investigation unit in the last 6 days. Do you finally understand the seriousness behind this issue finally?"

Karan did not know what to say.

"This goes a lot deeper than it seems boy. Understand the greater purpose behind it."

"And what is the greater purpose?"

"We aren't sure as yet. She knows better, and that's what

we're trying to find."

Kaushal then closed the file.

"Why are you afraid of involving the police or the Government into this? I mean they could find the truth easily. Just hand over her to them and let them decide what to do with her! Investigation isn't a job of your organization. Let the Police handle it then." Karan said.

"No. Once the student has taken admission in here, for 14 days we vouch for him or her. He or she is our property. We have been warned by the Government on a timely manner regarding this. Of course we don't want to waste our time investigating these matters, but we have no choice as we cannot approach the police or any government investigation authority without any concrete evidence."

"Why not?"

"It's complicated. Our lawyers tell us, that we cannot accuse someone of any crime without any prime evidence or the crime being committed. Our organization is a very reputed now. Not only here, but abroad too. Seminars are conducted only twice abroad and about four times here in India in a year. But the amount of revenue that we generate abroad in a single tour is twice that of we get here in India in all four sessions held round the year. We registering a baseless case against Richa or whoever is working with her would mean that she might go to the court against us. This would turn out to be much of a boomerang. We wouldn't be allowed to tour abroad and the Government might impose a temporary ban on our organization till the case is resolved. And you know at what pace the cases are settled in India. Plus the media, I don't even want to say anything about that!"

"But you people did find the audio-transmitter in her locker didn't you? Isn't that evidence?"

"It is, but who says it's hers other than us? She'll deny it. We need stronger evidence, which points directly to her. In case she's up to something."

"But why do you think that the Government will take such drastic steps against your organization in a case of mere spying by a young girl?"

"We fear that she isn't just an innocent young girl, spying or conducting an expose against us for some News Agency." Kaushal said.

"Then?"

"Ever heard what a 'sleeper cell' is?" Kaushal shot back a question to answer Karan's question.

"No. What are sleeper-cells?"

"Sleeper cells are people, basically terrorists who migrate long distances to somewhere they want to carry out a major operation. They aren't like other terrorists who just sneak into your city and start the chaos and killing. These sleeper cells stay basically in an unknown city, like for 8-10 years. They create their own identity in there. Work like normal people, earn a living, get married, and basically gel into the city so perfectly just like any person born and brought up there. And then one fine day they merge up with the other 'sleeper-cell' members and plan their once-in-a-life-time attack. Which more or less is their first and the last operation. So—."

"You are nuts!!" Karan couldn't listen to it anymore.

"Listen, we already had a Government intelligence report regarding such possible infiltration in our camp on a regular basis. We never took it seriously until we found that audio transmitter in Richa's locker. I know relating her to the sleeper-cell etc seems a bit over the top. But we work on whatever inputs we get from the intelligence agencies which monitors sensitive areas and organizations closely from time to time. I'm not saying she's one of those, but it is a possibility, she might have some other local criminal links or she might even be really up to something harmless."

"Or she might really be the one who she claims to be! A normal person working as an intern?"

"Karan, a normal intern journalist does not have fake IDs and collaborations with reputed NGO certificates forged, believe me. It isn't a joke!"

Karan now got up from his chair.

"You think I will really fall for all this stupid acts you made up?" He was now literally shouting at Kaushal. The security guards moved closer to him, but Kaushal signaled them to stop.

Kaushal then said, "See boy, all we were trying here were to take your friends' help in tracking down the truth. It's as simple as that. And now that he has switched sides, it's time you help us and help him indirectly."

"This is it. I'm done with you Sir. You can do whatever you want to me. There's no way going to fall for all your made-up fantasy stories and get brainwashed." Karan was firm.

"Okay then. Let him go." Kaushal finally said as he picked up his cell phone and began dialing some number.

The security guards moved two steps away from Karan. Karan didn't move. He just stared at Kaushal dialing the number.

"What are you doing?" Karan asked Kaushal.

Kausal paused as he said, "Calling the Police, CID to be precise. With no one co-operating with us we are left with no choice but to take some police help. Some things are to be done even if you don't like them. It's just like cleaning and dusting your house; you don't want to do it very often, but it's essential, boy."

"To report about Richa?"

"Of course. But you know what will happen next? They will hunt Richa and your friend down today or tomorrow. Then if in case she is involved in something serious as I told you and I hope she isn't, your friend will eventually be accused of covering it. Then your lives will turn to hell. You would be expelled from the college, blacklisted by other colleges. No company would hire you. Even if you aren't framed with any charges, when you would be out the jail after serving your sentence for 'helping' a criminal, it wouldn't do you any good. Society is brutal. You'll always be criminals in their minds. Always."

Karan stood quietly. Kaushal didn't say a word for next 10-15 seconds.

"You may go, you're free." Kaushal said again, as he picked up his phone again to dial his number.

Karan was very sure what his friend Vishal was doing was the right thing but even if there had been an iota of truth in Kaushal's story, it could ruin Vishal forever. After all, they hadn't really found anything concrete against the organization. Nor had the organization found anything definite against Richa, other than the audio-transmitter.

'If only I could know what Richa and Vishal were doing right now, what they had found out' Karan thought.

He was in two minds now. He had started to believe both sides of the story now. He wasn't ready to take chances.

"What do you want from me Sir!" Karan said, he wasn't sure what to do now.

Kaushal got up from his chair and placed his hand on Karan's shoulder as he spoke in a soft voice, "I understand your situation boy. But this just needs to be done. All I want you to do is help us. Tell us where they are and we will confront them with the reality and seek the truth. This way if Richa is guilty, Vishal will understand and you both would in fact be projected as our helpers rather than Richa's. And in case Richa is not guilty, there aren't any issues!"

"And what if you are guilty?" Karan shot back

"Hang us! Son, if we were guilty even a bit, believe me, we would've taken care of everything long time back. Making a girl and two guys disappear isn't a big deal you see! We had you people for like seven days with us now. Why didn't we take any action? Because we aren't that kind of people!"

Kaushal made sense. Karan thought for a minute.

"If I even tell you their location, and we go there? What

next? How do we confront Richa? How do we know the right from the wrong?"

Kaushal smiled, "Well, there's a new development that's happened about two hours ago. We've found something. We just need to get to them now. And you'll see for yourself"

"What do you mean?"

"You've already known too much. You'll see for yourself." Kaushal said

"Vishal has that advanced GPS tracking device with him, I mean the ID-Card you gave us. Why don't you just track them using it?" Karan asked.

To this Kaushal began to laugh uncontrollably and clapped a couple of times.

"So you guys really fell for it!?" he continued the laugh.

Karan had a puzzled expression.

"My son, in which world do you live? Advanced GPS tracker in a card-board paper thin ID-Card, that too in a personality development workshop? I thought it wouldn't work, but glad you guys fell for it. I just lied about it to Vishal just to make him conscious of his moves and not attempt any mischief. But if he has shared the idea with that smart chick girlfriend of his, she has probably got rid of that little cardboard thing somehow, to make his mind free without fear of getting tracked down."

Karan shook his head in dismay, "Sir, what do you want?"

"The location. Where are they?" Kaushal stared into Karan's eyes.

"Okay, But I won't tell you where they are unless you take me with you. I will take you there. They were to visit a couple of places since the morning, but it's kind of late afternoon, and by now I guess they must've reached their final destination." Karan said.

"Fair enough, now let's not waste any more time!" Kaushal patted Karan on his back, "Let's go!"

CHAPTER THIRTY TWO

About 2 hours ago,
12:45pm
Nearby Place C

Richa and I had walked for about half an hour now. We were cautious enough to check if anyone were following us. Though I was sure of Kaushal not sending any of the guys behind us thinking I'm with them, Richa wasn't sure and did not want to take any chances.

So basically we were on high-alert from the time since we had left the camp.

"You know what time it is?" Richa asked.

I looked at my wrist watch, "12.45 pm." I said.

"No." she said, "It's time to have lunch. I'm hungry."

'Great' I thought. I had lost all my appetite while on the mission that could make or break us in some way or the other and Ms. Richa was hungry just like 5-6 hours after a heavy breakfast.

"Ok. Let's find some good restaurant nearby and we'll eat there" I told her.

"No."

"Why?"

"We well have our food packed and eat somewhere else where we get place."

"And why would we do that?"

"Because sitting and eating at a restaurant would mean that we would be at the same place for at least like an hour or so, and that is dangerous. We have to be constantly on the move till we reach our destination. In case we are being physically followed or Kaushal has sent a search party, all we will do by staying at a place for a certain amount of time is give them enough buffer-time to catch up with us!"

I found it strange, but did not argue. We found a bakery from where we took a pack of 6 cup-cakes and sandwiches.

"Get one of those too, please. We'll have it while walking. I'm just too hungry to wait till we reach a proper place." Richa said as she pointed a tomato flavored jumbo *Lays* packet. I got two of those in my hand while we had our lunch packed in a plastic bag and started walking.

Richa took a packet of *Lays* from my hand and opened it as we kept on walking. I helped myself from mine.

We munched on the salted tomato-flavored wafers as we walked on. I watched Richa, she munched on hungrily. Such innocent and pretty she seemed. I could not even begin to imagine that such innocent creations of God would do anything like what Kaushal had told me earlier. She was just doing her job. Also, what could a mere teenager do after all? She wore jeans and a t-shirt. Her hair was left loose with which the wind occasionally played. Whenever I had time to observe her, all that came into my mind was just a word, 'beautiful'. That's it. She was an epitome of beauty.

"What are you looking at?" she asked me as she sensed that I was staring at her.

"Nothing." I smiled and shook my head.

She hit me again on the arm as she giggled, "*Dumbo!*"

About an hour later, we came finally to the lodge; that was

marked as *Place C* on the map. We stood outside the compounds as I took a deep breath.

"So this is it?" I asked.

"Yes, the map says so." Richa answered.

"Let's get in then!" I said.

"Yes."

"And what do we do once we get in?" I asked.

"Wait."

"Wait for?"

"Karan to show up with my agency people, remember?" Richa said raising an eyebrow, "Once those agency people are here, we are off duty and they will search the lodge for evidences or stuff. They might even bring the police along if they have a strong feel of finding something. Having the police on our side makes things a lot easier you know."

"You are forgetting something." I told her

"What?"

"There's also a possibility of some event to happen here, as this place is not only marked, but marked with today's date. I agree that we're not sure of the exact date if it's today or already happened in the past as the year is missing, but there's a possibility right?"

"Hmm.." Richa said, "I agree, but we have to take a chance. This is our one shot at fate. We wouldn't have taken such a drastic step if everything had gone according to my plans and they hadn't been exposed to the fact that I was here to collect information on their criminal acts in the camp."

I agreed with her. The finding of that electronic device (audio transmitter) at a place where even the iPods and cell-phones were banned, certainly gave away all of Richa's plans to the authorities.

"Come now." She said as she yet again held my hand and led the way. I walked behind her trying to keep up pace.

We now entered the reception area of the lodge. It was just like any other slightly-less-than- average lodges in the area. The reception area was mostly decorated by flower vases and a couple of random paintings hung behind the two receptionists, one of whom was busy on the phone.

Richa approached the other one.

"Good Morning, how may I help you?" the receptionist greeted us with a smile.

I wondered since when post 12 noon was considered as a morning? Either I heard her wrong or she belonged to a different time-zone right now, mentally at least if not physically.

"Yes Good afternoon" Richa smiled back and her 'good afternoon' greeting made the receptionist bite her tongue at her blunder as Richa said confidently "Mr. Kaushal from *A Way Around* has sent us here and told us to wait."

I had a lump in my throat. Certainly I hadn't seen this coming. It was probably one shot at getting out any kind of information from the receptionist to see if she was really waiting for someone.

"So soon?" the receptionist said as she pointed the wall clock, "But they won't be here till about late night. Around post 9 p.m. at least!"

There was a pause for about a couple of seconds, and then Richa promptly said, "Yes, I know, but we have been asked to wait."

"Okay. You seem new. What happened to Sammy? Isn't he coming to receive it here?" The receptionists further asked.

"No, we haven't been told much about what others do or not, Mr. Kaushal just asked us to wait here." Richa lied again.

"Okay, tell me the code then." , the receptionist smiled.

"What code?"

"O God, didn't Kaushal Sir mention to you the code? Like he does to every messenger who is supposed to stay here till he arrives with it! I cannot let you stay till I know that you know the code. I'm sorry, or I'll have to call Kaushal to confirm."

"NO! Don't call!" Richa almost shrieked. That one phone call made by the receptionist could've sent us right back where we started, in the hands of Kaushal and Co.

Neither Richa nor I had any idea of what the receptionist was saying to us. 'It' would be arriving post 9. At night 'it' would be here, some Sammy would be here too to collect 'it' late night. Kaushal had given codes to the people who were supposed to collect whatever would arrive here.

Richa just played along with the receptionist and now ended up at the point where we were supposed to cough up the 'code'.

"Why not? You do not have the code. I cannot let you stay. We don't know every messenger and receiver, the code is the only way we trust each other.", receptionists insisted.

"Don't call him. I mean, don't call him now. He has told us to tell you that he would be in an important meeting for the next couple of hours and he would not be liked to be disturbed by a call, may it be from anyone!" Richa blurted out. It was a lame made-up story. I wondered if the receptionist would fall for it.

"I don't believe you." the receptionist said.

"Okay then, go ahead. Don't say that I didn't tell you then." Richa spoke calmly avoiding eye contact with her.

The receptionist then pulled one of the four landlines in front of her towards herself and picked up the receiver. She held it for a moment next to her ear.

'This is it. We are doomed.' I thought

But just then she placed the receiver back where it belonged.

"Okay, here's the key. Go and wait, you're much too early." She said handing us a key to one of the rooms.

I couldn't believe our luck! Maybe this was a sign from God saying whatever we were up to, he was with us.

"By the ways, is there anything that could make us really believe that you have been sent by Kaushal?" the receptionist spoke again as she handed over the keys to us.

She had believed in us, but half heartedly. I wondered what we could do to make her believe that we were sent by Kaushal.

"I don't know about the code, but I remember there was

something we were given by Kaushal that might help you. Relax."
Richa spoke up.

"What?"

"Yes, Vishal, show it to them." Richa turned to me.

I gave her a 'show-them-what?' kind of questioning look. Before I could even answer or react to the situation, Richa came forward and reached my pant pockets and pulled out a piece of paper.

"This, here it is." Richa said.

It was the map that I still had in my pocket. She unfolded it and laid it right in front of the girl behind the desk.

"Oh! You have this! This is the code." the receptionist got excited as if she had just seen the most beautiful thing in the world, the cramped map.

"Is it?" I muttered which the receptionist heard.

She smiled, "Of course. I think they forgot to tell you that this is the code while handing this over to you!"

"Yes maybe, because Kaushal did say something regarding this, like if we don't get an access in here we were to show the map. I didn't know that this was a code though, or I guess we didn't hear properly" Richa sprang up with another lie. She was producing so many of them today. She was like a factory outlet for all of the lies spoken in the entire city today!

"All's well that ends well!". the receptionist said as she handed over the keys to me.

We took the keys and headed towards the stairs to the room allotted to us. Now all we had to do was wait, till Karan arrived with Richa's agency people and then at about 9pm, 'it' would arrive. Whatever 'it' was.

✳ ✳ ✳

Soon after Vishal and Richa left for their room, the second receptionist by the phone was free.

"What was that? Is something wrong?" She asked the first one, who had dealt with Vishal and Richa.

"They have the map."

"You're kidding me! We should let Kaushal know this!"

"I know. They seem dangerous. No one carries the map with them! They didn't have the code either, I somehow managed to fool them that the map was the code and that now we believe them."

"Why did you do that? We could've called Kaushal right here and got them captured."

"I know, but they could've escaped if we did so. Plus we don't know if they are here with some backup or something. Now, they're relaxed thinking that they've managed to fool us."

"Smart ehh!"

The first receptionist picked up the phone and dialed the number to Kaushal's cell-phone.

After three rings he picked up the call.

"Hello"

"Sir, it's me. The girl and a guy have reached here, with the map!"

"I know, I'm heading there with a friend of theirs. Just make sure they don't leave."

"Sure sir, I have them waiting in the room upstairs."

"Good."

There was a click as the conversation ended.

The two receptionists looked at each other and smiled. They knew they would be awarded for this. They knew that Kaushal would be proud of them now. The people that were up against the organization and Kaushal were up there in there lodge, waiting.

Waiting for their fate to take its most ugly turn of all times.

CHAPTER THIRTY THREE

About an hour later,
At the lodge

"So tell me, when are we killing this suspense?" I asked Richa waving the secret box at her.

"I guess you'll know for yourself." She avoided the answer, as always.

We now sat on the floor of the room on the second level of the lodge with our backs resting against the walls. It was quite strange, that the room had no bed, wardrobes or anything that a normal room in other lodges would have. It was plain simple room with a separate toilet-bathroom a wall clock and a calendar.

"Will you just keep that thing away Vishal, we might expect some uninvited guests now. I don't want them to lay their hands on it." Richa said. "No. I have to know now. It feels stupid carrying this thing all over without knowing how to open and access it! And yes, even if the guests lay their hands on this one, what would they get? Nobody knows the password but you! Not even me, for whom the box is intended!" I was frustrated. "Shhh! don't scream!" Richa placed her hand on my mouth, "Do you want to debate on it now!"

I composed myself.

"Richa, I think I am going crazy, all this we have gone through, is it even worth it? You have to tell me."

"I will. Soon enough." Richa consoled me, "Now do one thing, place the box somewhere such that no one finds it with us. We'll carry it with us afterwards."

"Afterwards? When?" I asked.

"When all this is over." she answered, "We have no idea as to what all will take place here now in some time. The box going in the wrong hands is the last thing I want to happen."

"No Richa, I have trusted you blindly for a bit too long now. I have to know what is in it."

Richa took a deep breath and paused for a couple of seconds.

"So you really want to know?"

"Yes"

"What if I tell you it was nothing but just a prank?"

"Oh God, Richa, now you're doing this to cover up the truth! Why would you play a prank such stupid as this?"

"To boost your confidence."

"What?"

"You were always this low self-esteemed, low confidence guy and the time you had to take a bold decision or step outside your boundaries, you needed a push and a hell lot of convincing! Like the escape, like the spying thing in the store room, like this second escape. You're always so hard to convince unless you know there's a backup plan!"

"Okay , so?" I interrupted.

"So this box was nothing but my way of making you somehow believe that no matter what, you have a backup when there's nowhere else to go!"

"Seriously Richa, what the fuck is wrong with you?!" I screamed.

"Don't you dare use that word with me!" Richa dared me.

"If this wasn't for real, I will break this box here itself!"

I said as I raised my hand to throw the box away.

"NO!" Richa sprang into action to hold my hand from doing whatever I was trying to do.

"Why not?"

"Because I say so!" Richa now snatched the box away from me. "If it was nothing more than a prank, then why the need to hide it now?" I shot my second uncomfortable question to her.

"Because.." Richa hesitated, "Because,

it's of some sentimental value to me."

I paused for a second and then applauded sarcastically, "You're really smart Richa. I wonder how you manage to come up with a lie so fast every single time."

"Okay enough fun now. Let's hide this." She got up on the floor and glanced around.

"Listen Richa, why do you have to be so mysterious all the time? Have I not gained enough trust from you. Do you think I still don't deserve to know everything that I need to know?" I asked her as I got up.

She didn't answer. She was still busy searching for a hiding place for that stupid box.

"For the time being, we'll hide it behind the commode flush tank in the toilet." She said as she walked inside the toilet.

The commode flush-tank was situated at a certain height, so Richa had to close the commode lid and stand on it to reach her destination. I watched in silence.

Then we came back to the room and sat on the floor.

"I'm tired." Richa said as she lay down on the floor looking at the ceiling.

I lay down beside her. There was total peace. No noise, no sound.

We both silently stared at the ceiling above trying to make sense of everything that had happened till now in our own minds. I was worried about the future. What would happen in a few hours was unknown to us. What had happened earlier all these days in the camp felt like a dream. And that box. I knew it had something that I should know, and it wasn't a prank for sure. What Richa had did right now, whatever she explained to me right now about it, THAT was a prank. If only I could guess the password somehow. I thought the only option left for me to find out about the box was wait and watch till all this got over.

"You know Richa—." I began to say as I turned towards her. But she was fast asleep.

I stared at her beautiful face. So calm and composed, so strong. As always.

I then lay on my back completely and closed my eyes too. I was so tired. I too, fell asleep in 5 minutes.

✵ ✵ ✵

"Vishal! Wake up! I guess they're here!"

It was Richa. I woke up instantly and glanced at the wall clock. It was 5.45pm. We were asleep for about 2 hours it seemed. At least I was. I had no idea when Richa had got up.

I sat up straight.

"What happened?"

"Shhh! They're here."

We listened quietly; there was noise and commotion outside. A bunch of people were taking the wooden stairs to the lobby and approaching our floor.

"I guess this is it." said Richa.

I took a deep breath and held her hand.

The voices grew louder and suddenly they stopped right outside our door.

And then, there was knocking.

"Who is there?" Richa asked.

"Your friends my fellows."

"These surely aren't my people; I hope Karan has brought in the right guys!" Richa whispered.

"Friends who?" I asked without opening the door.

No one answered. With a thud there was a strong hit on the door. And then another one, that broke its lock.

Karan stood outside and stared at us from there. He wasn't smiling.

"Ohh it's you. What's wrong with—." I couldn't complete my sentence when another three figures came into the room from behind Karan. Kaushal along with his two bodyguards.

"Shit shit shit!!" Richa gasped as she sensed the situation. The plan had failed.

"This isn't any shit lady." Kaushal said with a wicked smile, "Fasten your seat-belts kids. It's showtime!"

CHAPTER THIRTY FOUR

Kaushals' wicked smile was back again. Dramatically he made his way in front as he walked up to us.

"Hello love birds, good afternoon. How's life?" he said sarcastically. His smile went off slowly as I could clearly see the rage in his eyes staring down at us.

Richa and I got up. I looked at her, she was shocked. Not because Kaushal had turned up here, but it was Karan who had led him here.

"Dude, your friend cheated us!" She said to me. Her voice cracked with a mixture of anger and disappointment while she said it.

I did not know how to respond to this.

"Okay I can explain, and there is no need to be tense or scared…" Karan began to explain but was 'shh-ed' by a hand gesture of Kaushal.

"That's enough. Karan, you may leave now. And thanks for leading us to this place. We'll take it from here." Kaushal said without even looking back at Karan.

Karan was shocked by the sudden change of tone and body language of Kaushal. He realized that he had been used and

208 ⚬ *The Other Way Round*

cheated by Kaushal.

"No, I will stay till my friends are here." Karan didn't move from his place.

"Okay. Your choice, not mine." Kaushal shrugged.

Kaushal now turned to Richa who was furious with anger, "So tell me, how much they are paying you for this? What all you have against us till now? Let's sort it out."

"Shut up!", Richa shot back.

"Whoa.. Little miss angry young woman!" Kaushal laughed.

I had a strong feeling this could get really ugly.

Richa just ignored Kaushal's evil laugh and narrowed her eyes towards Karan as she questioned him, "Did you make that call to my agency? They're coming aren't they?"

"Err.. actually Richa, I swallowed the chit and—."

Before even Karan could answer that question, Kaushal spoke up, "No he didn't. No one is coming for you. Because if they do, we'll be out!"

Kaushal's tone had suddenly changed like I had never seen before. His appearance wasn't friendly either.

"Sir! What are you up to?" Karan was confused now as he couldn't believe the horror that he had been brainwashed so easily by Kaushal and had acted against his friends, "I thought we were here to sort things out and find the truth!"

Kaushal once again dramatically turned towards him as he spoke with the same evil smile on his face, "Boy, of course we're here to sort things out. But our way, not yours."

"I had told you people to believe me!" Richa looked at Karan with her eyes watery now. She couldn't take what she thought of as 'betrayal' by Karan towards us. I was confident that Karan must have done this solely because he was brainwashed by Kaushal.

"Everything I did till now, everything your friend Vishal risked till now is gone. We've lost it." Richa continued pointing towards Karan, "We've lost it stupid!"

I placed my hand over her shoulder to calm her. She was

outraged and full of emotions.

"You don't understand Vishal, you have no idea what these people are up to. Their racket is much deeper and stronger than we can possibly imagine!" she went on.

"I'm afraid to admit guys, but your girl is right!" Kaushal said teasing us.

Karan and I just couldn't believe what we had just heard. Kaushal had almost laid out the truth in front of us. We now knew the black from the white.

"You aren't getting away this time." Richa was furious.

"Whoa I'm so scared!" Kaushal said acting scared as he laughed even more, "Dear Miss Richa, you have to understand that you do not have anything against us."

"Well a witness is enough. And there are three!" Richa shot back

"And who will believe you? The court asks for evidence, and that you do not have against us! Rather we have quite a few evidences against you. You trespassed our private property, planted our camp with your stupid audio transmitters and stuff in order to conduct an illegal sting operation!"

"Well you'll see." Richa was confident.

"What?"

"Do not think we don't have anything against you." Richa continued, "That specialized ID-cards you gave us? With your advanced GPS transmitter installed in it, we still have it, even if not with us right now, can be traced by the police."

"Oh c'mon you kids! We tell you something and you believe it?" Kaushal said, "Those are just plain normal ID cards! Just like any other student around the camp has! We just made you believe that those had something high tech in them so that we wouldn't have to keep constant watch on you while you were in the camp, because you wouldn't try anything funny thinking you being monitored."

Richa were dumbstruck by the revelations given by Kaushal

now, Karan just nodded from behind with his eyes glued to the floor.

"Actually you know what, I'll let you know what actually happens in *A Way Around.*" Kaushal smiled at us.

"And why would you do that?" Karan asked.

"Do what?"

"I mean why would you tell us what happens in there?"

Kaushal patted on Karan's shoulder before answering, "Boy, it doesn't really matter you see. You're just a bunch of kids, you have nothing against us as evidence and even if you did, we know how to handle it. Also, I really admire all the bullshit effort you kids made to collect evidences and stuff against us. You deserve to hear the truth, but you don't deserve to preach it. I'm a sport too!"

I was bewildered. All this seemed like a nightmare to me. Kaushal then walk past his two huge body guards and Karan as he shut the door close behind him.

"Let's start from the beginning." He said rubbing his hands together as he began his story.

"I was born in a small village near east Maharashtra in a very poor family. I come from a very poor background, and we had this land of ours on which we would cultivate crops, basically sugarcane for a living that didn't go well. Father had passed away when I was young and it was entirely due to my mother that I had the privilege of completing my education. My mother was everything to me and I was everything to her. After graduation, I never left my village to search for a job only because my mother would not leave her village and I could not leave her. I was always a shy and awkward kind of a guy with very few friends and their number became even smaller as they left for bigger cities in search of further opportunities, I could talk to people but could never make enough friends. Back then, all I did was work in the farm and serve my mother. We were a very happy little family. As I had

no brother or sister, my mother was my only friend. Our other relatives had already abandoned my mother blaming her for my father's death for no reason. My mother always insisted that I should go out to the city and look for a proper job, get married and enjoy life as other kids of my age did, but I never listened to her. I did not want to leave her alone there. Soon with age her health started getting bad and during an epidemic of viral fever in our village, my mother passed away. It came as a massive shock to me. My mother, my only friend, philosopher and guide was no more and it seemed that I had nothing to look forward in my life. I often thought of committing suicide but the very thought of cutting my own wrist or hanging by the ceiling fan sent tremors through my spine. I would often think of my mother when such thoughts dominated my mind. I desperately needed a distraction and a new life to get out of that emotional trauma of my life. One fine day, I saw an advertisement of this workshop being held in a nearby place for 14 days. I attended this workshop just like that. It was due to this workshop of Mr. Rathod that I began to see the world outside my village; I learnt that there was so much to see, so much to learn and so much to take from the outside world. I understood what I had missed in my entire life due to never stepping outside my village. For the first time ever, I came in contact with the people outside my village. All this began when A Way Around was just beginning to grow big. I joined this esteemed organization after attending two sessions of 14 days each back to back about a couple of years back, so inspired was I by them. I had found a new dimension to life, a new way of looking at life. And then I attended one more of their seminars. Mr. Rathod soon saw my interest in their organization and invited me to be a part of it on a regular basis rather than a student. I was thrilled. It was like a dream come true. Now not only I could roam and see the entire country or tour the world with them, but I could even help people like me attending the workshop! Everything was going well. I felt as if I had those things that I missed in my entire life. Interaction with people from all walks of life, all parts of the globe, frequent visits to countries whose mere locations on the globe I was not even aware of a while ago. But then I met some other kind of people too. There was this friend of mine who I had met during a course in Hyderabad. He asked me to carry a packet of his 'medicine' with me the next time I toured Europe for his friend. When asked why just he couldn't courier it or visit the friend himself, he told me that he couldn't go due to some visa problems and couriering was no option as I was anyways going and he wanted to ensure that his friend got the medicine personally. My friend back then had asked me to be careful about the packet as the medicine was banned in Europe, so I carried it with my personal baggage rather than the common one. The entire A Way Around team was having a 14 day session in Amsterdam the very next month. A group of 35 students and 17 staff members flew to the city of Amsterdam. Mr. Rathod, by then was a global phenomenon and a well known figure and had a VVIP pass. Which meant that these people were not frisked as thoroughly as others were. Also, I being very close to him was saved of the trouble too. Only on delivering the medicine packet to the address my friend had given me, I understood that I was being just a delivery man for a drug-packet! On returning to India I had a fight with him for misusing me and my status in the camp to do his personal and illegal drug-trafficking. He then apologized to me saying that it was urgent and he would not do it again. He did pay me for the job done. The amount was so huge that I had never even had written that many zeros after a digit even on a paper in my entire life! I was amazed, even though I was against it back then, I couldn't fathom the fact that mere transfer of a few packets could mean so much in terms of money. That is when it all began to disintegrate. My moral values took a U-turn as I teamed up with him to form a network. Later I did parcel out some more packets to some more countries. Within a year, I had the money that I would've taken hundreds of years to earn had it been done in a legal way. But then laws tightened after the infamous 9/11 attacks happened and nothing was as easy as it was earlier. The customs even if they were getting their due pays under the table, wouldn't let us go and allow the transfer of prohibited materials into their respective countries. Also, soon enough the rumors of some 'illegal activities' and 'drug-trafficking' in A Way Around surfaced were doing the rounds and the media took up the issue. But without evidence and power of organization it was suppressed without creating much havoc.

We soon decided to take a break from it and took a decision to limit our activities within our own country for a while. I then formed my own personal networks in here and as A Way Around made a country-wide tour; I made my own tour along with it. It was just perfect. The workshop didn't last for more than 14 days at any particular place, was constantly on the move and was very much respected and roamed about to nooks and corners of the country. Nobody would suspect us. I have been running a parallel organization within an organization like this for the last few years I guess!"

Kaushal paused. There was pin drop silence in the entire room as Kaushal stood in between Karan and me as I watched him narrate him his story. The bodyguards stood near the closed door.

"You are evil! So evil!" Karan exclaimed.

"Not that I'm complaining!" Kaushal laughed and then he turned back towards his guards, "Okay, frisk them. See what they've got."

The guard came forward as he began frisking us one by one.

Kaushal spoke, "See people, I'm not a bad person, I won't hurt you. After this frisking and knowing that I have no threat from you guys, I'm just going to let you go. We are not murderers or extortionists, just smugglers as some people might call us. We just supply to people their 'medicines' that makes them happy." he further added putting on a cheerful expression.

"Believe me. My agency won't leave you. If you try to hurt us or.." Richa began

"Whoa! Chill there girl!" Kaushal interrupted, "Who said anyone was going to hurt you? We just want to make sure you people do not have any hard evidence against us and we'll let you go! I don't care what you bark out once you go out of here, simply because speech doesn't mean anything outside without a proof! Many like you from other private organizations or press have come and gone before, no one could prove anything. And the one who tried or managed to get the evidence and refused to surrender, never returned. They're cases are still pending in the police stations in some file named as 'Missing Persons Report'. We are bigger now, and more powerful than you can possibly imagine. Almost close to half of the government and custom officials literally tie-up with us. Trust me, you cannot go far. You are no threat to us as long as you don't have anything."

The guards by now had finished frisking us.

"Sir, it's just these things that we've found" said one of those buffalo-sized guards displaying our wallets, cell-phones, money and digital camera.

"Get them here" Kaushal asked the guards to hand him over the camera and other things.

One by one he opened the back of the cell-phones as he removed the sim-card from each.

He twisted it 2-3 times in opposite directions trying to bend it and eventually ended up breaking it.

Richa clenched her teeth as she looked at Kaushal; but he did not budge.

"Now that you've learned about this, I will have to change the way my network works again." He smiled.

He then observed the expression all three of us had on our faces. Seeing us confused at what he had just said he gave an explanation, "Oh, you know as I already have told you, I run an organization within an organization. And just like any other successful organization, mine too has a set of rules and regulations and methodologies of working. This organization helps me travel the country and enables me to carry out my operations and handle various networks around it in a secretive manner. I develop my own methods of working and change them every time on a frequent basis. This method was one of them."

"I don't get it" Richa said.

"You won't. At least not till I explain." Kaushal proudly said, as he continued with his explanation, "So as I said, for every operation of mine, I need to ensure complete secrecy and a chain of people to carry it out without even them having complete knowledge about the plan and the people involved. Basically for my trafficking, all I need is a 'client' and a 'supplier'. I'm just the one who plays the *connecting-the-dots* kind of game between them due to my influences and stuff. I develop a unique plan for a certain period of time, and then work on another, the suppliers and transporters change too, every time. This indigenous plan devised by me is revised every time and runs parallel to the actual workshop. The place that you probably could have visited first, *place A,* according to the map I mean, is a barren land and is owned by me. Now on receiving request for certain amount of packets, I find my suppliers. These 'suppliers' are the people who provide me with the various drug-packets and the 'clients' are the ones who demand it. My work is to act as a chain or like a Fed-Ex agent without either of them knowing who the other is. What the supplier does is he receives money in cash from our agents and delivers the packets into the lockers at a private bank at Place B. What happens now is, the supplier makes the packet deposit in the lockers at the Bank at place B under the name he wishes to and sets a unique password to it, which is a random 4-digit number. Now, as a part of a plan he now purchases an ordinary sim-card on a temporary basis. He then saves the name by which the locker is booked and the password that he has set for the locker in the drafts in sim-memory of that card. Now all he as to do is place the card somewhere. So, with a bunch of his friends he is set out on a camping trip just like any other tourists.

Place the card where the next person in the chain would find it. In this case, he was given a place for 'camping purpose' for a night in that barren land at place-A. Now during the camping session at the Place A, he buries the sim-card there and marks the place accordingly. Then, we send some of our people that we call as 'new agent' to just collect the sim-card from there, and then receive the packets from the Bank locker by providing the name and password to the bank authority. You must have noticed here, that neither the supplier is aware of who collects the sim from the place, nor is the collector that is the 'new agent' given any idea how the card was buried there and by who. Now once this packet is received, our 'new agent' arrives here at this lodge. He places the packets here, stays for a day and then leaves. Before leaving he chooses his own set of 4-digit password for the next agent tells the newly decided password to the receptionists. Then on the last day, we come here and collect the packets and deliver it to the clients."

Kaushal paused again. My head had started to spin.

"You know what the benefits of doing all this are?" Kaushal boasted

None of us answered. None of us were even interested.

"Well, you don't ask question here when I want you to!" he said sarcastically as he added, "The benefits are, no one really knows in the system I explained to you that who works for who. The client and the supplier are totally cut off from each other due to the numerous chain-agents in between! Even if a particular agent is caught in the middle, he has no clue how this chain actually started or where it ended. All the first agent did was receiving cash from us and delivered the packet in the bank and left a password. But he has no idea as to who he was supplying or even who would be next to receive the code and retrieve the packet from the bank locker. The same with the 'new agent', that is agent number two. All he does is receive the hidden sim-card from the place we instruct him to, and takes the packet from the bank-locker by providing the password saved in the sim and gives it here. He doesn't know who placed the sim-card at place-B nor does he know who will receive it from here! In both scenarios not even one of them knows how long this chain is while they are transferring packets as all they deal with is codes and passwords."

"And what happens after the 'new agent' places the packet here in the lodge by giving the receptionist another set of code?" I hesitated, but asked.

"Did I not tell you that we, rather I myself collect it from here? I then give it to my client who had given me the money in the first place. This is what I call total disconnect from the client to supplier. It's just me, and my method. This of course changes every time and now that you people have discovered it, I'll change the very next time. Don't feel bad for it you see, I'm pretty sharp at making plans and mazes." he teased us.

"And how do you know the codes that the first person and the new agent had chosen? In order to collect the packet, what do you do?" Richa asked

"Well, we don't have to know the code; this is my staff over here. I just come here and they hand me over the packet. The code is set by the final agent at the lodge while depositing is done as procedure set by my plan. You see, we make people believe a hell of a lot of things that aren't really there, for our own benefit. Hence we make the last delivery person; our end supplier set a code too. This makes him think that there are more people in the chain and they in turn would access his code somehow to further transfer the deal. These basic principles help me conceal the exact number of agents, clients and suppliers from each other."

He then took out a carry bag from his pocket and placed all our belongings that the guards had confiscated from us into it.

"Okay enough *gyaan* you had for the day. Leave now." He said as one of the guards reached for the locked door handle.

"We need our things back." Richa demanded.

"Not possible. I'm leaving you un-harmed and with so much

information. And you want your stupid things back? What sort of people are you? The *Oh-please-kill-me-now* kind?" Kaushal mocked.

"We'll go to the police." I said

"Please do. And tell them I said 'Hi'." Kaushal smiled.

Nobody moved in the room.

"See we need to end this deadlock. So I'm leaving. You may stay as long as you wish." Kaushal turned away.

"We cannot let him go!" Richa with her eyes widened screamed at me and Karan.

With an instant Karan sprang up to his feet and jumped on Kaushal by setting his grip on his neck. Kaushal collapsed on the ground struggling for air. Within a fraction of second one of the two guards grabbed Karan by his hair with just one hand and pulled him off Kaushal.

With some coughing and struggle to take initial breath, Kaushal got up on his feet.

"Why are you guys making this ugly? You're just a bunch of college kids, and I don't want to be harsh with you! Cannot you just leave and let us do our jobs?" Kaushal was screaming furiously now.

Then there was a loud noise. Noise that of a slap. The guards hand had made a good contact with Karan's cheek. With a thud Karan collapsed on the ground and started bleeding from his mouth. The other guard raced towards Richa and held her from behind. She tried her best to get out of his grip but couldn't move a bit. It looked just like a fish caught by its tail in hand who flutters with all its power but is helplessly in between the strong hold of fisherman's mere two fingers.

Kaushal then walked up to Richa as I looked in horror. He reached his pocket and came out with a small Swiss-knife-like weapon.

"Seriously guys, if you want to fight it out, I'm ready. Don't test my patience."

"Don't!" I screamed, "Don't hurt her!

Karan needs medical attention. Spare us and we guarantee you no harm done to you from our side." Kaushal laughed again. This time louder than all the three-four times he already had done earlier.

"Well to start with, you people cannot even harm us if you even want to. All I wanted now is to you to leave peacefully from here." He said as he went closer to Richa.

Richa struggled more as he approached her.

"Wait.. wait!" I went towards Kaushal, and just then the guard who had made Karan fall flat on the floor held me tight and dragged me in another corner.

Karan now moved on the floor as he became conscious of the situation again. He moved and moaned with pain, but did not get up on his feet.

"No.. do not hurt them, I guarantee. Peace." He moaned

"See? That's called smartness." Kaushal pointed to the crawling creature on the floor.

And within a split of a second, just like any Hindi film heroine would do, Richa spat on our villain, Kaushal's face.

With an instant reflex and anger, Kaushal slapped her back. I watched as the guard holding me held me even tighter sensing I would fight hard now to get away. It was a slap alright but something made me feel it was serious. Kaushal looked scared after he did so. Richa's face was covered due to Kaushal standing in the way of my view.

"Take him away from here fast!" Kaushal ordered the guard holding me.

"Shit shit shit!!" Karan on the floor gasped as he saw at Richa.

When the guard started dragging me out of the room I finally saw Richa. Her face was covered with blood! The guard behind her held her strongly but she was now motionless in his hands with her face fully covered in blood. I was shocked, and terrified at the same time! I couldn't fathom the fact that a mere slap, however hard it may be, could result in so much bloodshed? I glanced at Kaushal's hands. Now I got it. He still held the pen-knife in his hand that he had used to slap Richa. In the rage and anger filled with humiliation he had completely forgot he carried a weapon in his hand and slapped her with it!

With all the energy I possibly had, I gave a push to the guard holding me and managed to get out of his grip. I ran for the door and opened it.

"I'm calling the police! Richa was right! You are so evil and won't stop at anything!" I said as ran past the lodge corridor up to the stairs.

"Leave her! Get him." Kaushal shrieked behind me to the guards. Within seconds I glanced from the corner of my eyes the two huge guards with thumping noises were charging behind. I took the stairs, skipping two steps at a time.

As soon as the receptionists saw the commotion, and me running towards the exit door, they reached for the main door and locked it before I even reached there. I ran towards it and 'click' it was locked from inside by one of the receptionist. She quickly ran back to a corner to watch what would happen next.

I was trapped. I turned back as I stood with my back resting on the locked door.

Kaushal in a very dramatic way, descended from the stairs too, clapping with both his hands as the guards cornered me.

"See what you did! Why the bloodshed?" he said.

I was furious, I glanced the entire reception area. A window beside the door was my only hope to get away now. I swiftly made my way towards the desk as I held the receptionist like a kidnapper would hold a hostage. I had no weapon, but I quickly scanned the desk and took up a small scissors placed there.

"Let me go or I'll harm her." I said. The other receptionists ran away far from us as I held her friend hostage.

"You think we care?" Kaushal said wickedly, "Don't let him go!"

Then the guard to my right did the unthinkable. He marched towards us without any hesitation.

"I'm telling you I'll hurt her!" I said.

"Oh shut up will you!" he said as he slapped me hard, freed away the lady from me and grabbed my throat. I was choking now.

"Get him upstairs, don't kill him!" Kaushal said

The guard loosened his grip on my throat and grabbed my shirt as we made our way towards the stairs again. I didn't know what Kaushal's next plan was. Within a minute we were up in the corridor again on the first floor.

I had a feeling that they would now kill all three of us and dump us somewhere. We were too dangerous to be let loose now. An instant chill ran through my spine on the very thought of getting murdered along with my friends. I couldn't take it.

I stopped midway as I held the corridor railing with my two hands tight.

"I'm not going anywhere you tell me to go." I said

I glanced behind me. I could still see the door was locked below and the receptionists were nowhere in view now. They were probably hiding somewhere now.

"Oh really? You don't think we cannot force you, do you?" Kaushal said looking at my grip on the railing.

I did not say a word. I just held the railing tighter so that they wouldn't succeed in taking me anywhere. The guards again held each of my hand and started pulling me away from the railing.

With their combined force, it shouldn't have taken them more than 10 seconds to get me out of there, but something gave me strength from within to stay there.

They tried for a minute and finally Kaushal couldn't resist the insult.

"Oh you're kidding me!" He said as he came forward and slapped me.

I didn't move. He slapped again. I still didn't move. Then with full force he furiously banged his head on my chest. I choked again and felt like all of my blood from my chest had rushed to my brain. I immediately let go off my grip on the railing as I lost control and held my chest with my hands. I was in total agony, and then came another blow from Kaushal. This one hit me harder than the first one. Within a split second, my back crashed with a thud on the railing behind me with force. The wooden railing cracked and I tripped off it.

"Get him, he's falling..!" these were the words that hit my ears just before I began to fall directly from the corridor to the reception area, some 40 feet below! A straight vertical fall.

I could see Kaushal and the guards staring down at me as I fell from above. A mere one or two seconds fall, but felt silent. Felt like one of those slow motioned shots in a movie. I closed my eyes and prepared for the worst to come. With a thud my back and my head simultaneously banged on the reception area floor. I thought it was over.

I opened my eyes; I saw Kaushal and the guards running down towards me using stairs.

I touched the back of my head with my hand as I lay down motionless. I didn't feel the pain. I saw my hand after I withdrew it from the back of my head. It was drenched in blood. I looked at the ceiling. It had started to spin now. With an instant, a cold chill and wave of pain passed right through my spine to my head as everything in front of me went from totally bright to fade to faint and then finally blank. I blacked out.

CHAPTER THIRTY FIVE

Present Day
At the hospital

Vishal stopped reading. There wasn't anything to read further. He closed the several word-documents and searched where the remaining part of the story was written. There wasn't any. It was clear that this was all he had written since the last time he was conscious in the hospital. He had been reading his own story for the last two hours or so. He looked around in dismay.

'So this is why I was being kept so secretive about this accident.' He thought.

He wondered where Richa would be right now and how Karan was so cool and calm about everything and covering up the truth, acting as if everything was normal and the accident was just like any other normal accident that occurs. It was clear from whatever he had read that the authorities at *A Way Around* were indeed very powerful and brought him and his friend to this stage and caused so much of trauma. Obviously Karan didn't want to take any further chances and probably wanted just to forget it all and move on with life thinking this life is a boon as we survived after being through so much. There was also the question of

Richa. Vishal had not been informed or even heard her name from Karan in the days since he had become conscious. The book indicated that she was more than just a friend and meant more to Vishal and it would be highly impossible for Karan just to forget mentioning her in their general talks.

Also, Vishal doubted whether Karan had even told her about him being out of coma now. If it were the case she would have called by now. Unless... Then the biggest fear gripped Vishal. 'Unless she herself was in some trouble even now!' Vishal thought, 'Was she okay? What did they do to her later? What was Karan hiding?'

The nurse had told him that Richa had visited him when he was in Coma, but it was kind of strange how she never called him nor Karan even mentioned her in their conversations in the last four days. Coincidence?

Too many questions bugged Vishal at once. His head had started to ache now.

Vishal closed the laptop, placed it aside and lay down on his bed. Within minutes, even though his mind was overflowing with thoughts, he went to sleep.

✳ ✳ ✳

"Hey buddy, how are you doing? Here's your dinner for today. And guess what, I've got your favorite sweet for today! *Rass Malaai* !" , it was Karan.

He entered the hospital room as he placed the parceled food in carry bags on the desk beside Vishals' desk.

Vishal had been waiting for this since the time he had read those self-written records of the camp happenings.

"Karan, can you please tell me now how exactly I ended up here." Vishal asked his friend.

"Can we eat first?" Karan said as untied the knots on the plastic carry bags which contained the food.

"No. Tell me first."

"The doctor has told me to not to put strain on your—."

"Forget the doctor. I don't give a shit! Tell me!" Vishal exploded

"Okay calm down!" Karan was now shocked by this sudden revolt, "What's the matter?"

"I read it."

"Read what?"

"Everything. Every single word. I know why and how we are here. I just want to know why you have been hiding this from me all this time!" Vishal finally blurted it out.

"Oh! That, you read it? I was about to remind you. So when are we publishing it?" Karan smiled.

Vishal didn't get a word of what Karan meant.

"What?" he asked.

"That book you were working on! You said you read it, and it was your dream to get it published! Now that you are fine, I guess we make some happy ending to it and look out for some good publishers!" Karan said.

"I don't get it. I don't understand what you trying to say!" Vishal's head started to spin again. It was as if both were communicating in different languages.

"Wait, let me explain to you." Karan said as he began to explain further:

"We had both decided; rather you had decided to go on that camp *A Way Around* for the documentary thing of yours. I joined in too. As you might know, it took a hell lot of convincing for us to the college and parents to skip a term for the Discovery contest! But then we went ahead with it. In the midst of it, when we were up to a field trip, there was a mishap wherein a girl, Richa, who was our friend and your 'crush' later, ran into trouble with certain goons. And you like a hero went all alone to protect her. But this not being any Hindi movie, our hero, that's you, got hit back pretty well. They bashed you with rods and sticks. But then Richa got a chance to run away. I tried to save you but they bashed up me too. Richa called the police by then and we were safe. The gang ran away before they arrived. You had severe cuts and bruises on head and your condition was quite serious since then. About two days later you came back to your consciousness and were getting better. Your head injury was severe and due to multiple fractures you were told to be bedridden for a couple of months. This is when you came up with the idea of writing a book! It was always that you wanted to be a writer and publish a book on fiction but never got the time to do so. When you had nothing to do much just than lie down and stare at the hospital ceiling, we came up with this idea. This had two benefits, one, that you finally didn't feel these days of lying down bedridden as a waste of time, and two, you would finally be living your dream of writing your book! Then the question about of the topic for the book aroused. We eventually concluded on fictionalizing our trip to *A Way Around* by adding some truth and lots of fiction to the story! We had planned well on for one hell of a thriller you see...! But while working on it, your problems with fits and frequent vomiting started as there was some swelling in your brain according to the doctors. You needed to be operated on soon. But you insisted on completing the book up to about at least 80% before going in for the operation. The rest 20% was left to me, but I always wanted you to finish it. And hence I'm still waiting for you to script its happy ending! But now that you've already read it, I guess we can discuss the proper ending! Quite exciting, no?"

Vishal had no clue as to what to think now.

"But we were there for our documentary for Discovery Channel! What are you telling me all this?"

"Yes we were. But then only one day prior to the *A Way Around* started, they called you to tell that there was a mistake and that you were in the 'waiting line' and not clearly shortlisted. But we had already planned with the camp thing anyways and taken permission from the college and parents after all the scolding so we couldn't tell them this and we went ahead with the camp anyways"

"You are making this up aren't you?" Vishal gave a straight questioning look to Karan.

"Why would I? I still have that letter from the Channel at my house. Are you crazy? You think all that you've written in there did happen exactly as it's been written?"

"Yes. I've never mentioned that rejection letter from the Discovery Channel in the book! There wasn't any! We were on an actual documentary mission which went horribly wrong as written in the book!"

"Yes we were there, agreed. But most of the things other than the characters and a few lecture inputs are fictionalized for the books' sake. One doesn't write everything as it happens while writing fiction!" Karan tried hard to explain.

"You really think I will believe such a made up story of yours, haan?" Vishal was skeptical.

"It's ridiculous of you to think that ways Vishy!" Karan was bewildered.

"Listen, there's nothing to be afraid of, Karan. I know these people are very powerful and influential, but we have got to do something and not just let it go like this! Don't make up stuff and try to convince me the opposite. You obviously must have been relaxed when I lost my memory and that now you could just play and act like nothing happened and it was easier to silence me. But unfortunately for you, I read this story of mine in my laptop and now I know. Tell me for once you're lying and also where Richa is."

"Dude, you need to calm down here." Karan said as he got up to fetch a glass of water for Vishal.

"Listen to me; I was here with you all the time you wrote that book in your laptop. I know every word, because it was our idea. And those things with *A Way Around* being caught in that smuggling racket and the girl being hurt in the end stuff. It's all made up! You really don't think it's for real do you? Because if you do, you're challenging your own intelligence. All of it was meant as purely fiction for some *masaala* in the story! The girl, Richa was the one you had a crush on in the entire camp and you both did go out the first time by sneaking out as written in there. But that was it! There was nothing more, nothing less."

"Where is she now?" Vishal demanded.

"Somewhere in her hometown Delhi! Safe and sound!" Karan answered.

"How do I believe you?" Vishal was still skeptical.

"You have to. I can prove it to you. I can prove it that all that written in the book never happened and that love-attraction whatever angle that we had put in that book with that Richa girl is fiction too! Even though Richa was our friend back in there, the story around you two is totally made up for some good fiction suspense and spice!"

Vishal shook his head in disagreement. He still refused to believe.

"You know what Vishal, your memory being totally washed out now is the most unfortunate thing for me since you've read that thing. Because if you hadn't lost your memory, you would know the truth and we would be quietly completing our book! Now I'm doing all this nonsense of convincing you of fact over fiction!" Karan concluded.

"Okay, so you want me to believe that our trip to the camp happened just as normal as to the other people back there? And all that suspense, thrill, smuggling racket story, the brutal end was made up to make a good fiction novel?"

"Of course! The problem here now is that you have read your own fiction story and ended up believing it to be true!"

"Prove it to me."

Karan paused. He was finally given time to prove his point.

"See, your 'biography' as you say has chapters such as those where in you weren't present in the scene when they happened! Like the conversation that apparently happened between Kaushal and me after you and Richa escaped the camp for the second time! How do you explain that? That chapter is there because I have written it!"

Vishal thought for a moment.

"Go ahead, I'm listening" Vishal said.

Karan went on, "Also, if I ever feared of you finding out the truth, I would have easily deleted those documents from your laptop in the last two days! But I didn't do that, because it doesn't matter! It isn't the truth. It's just a book and not your life. You won't understand it unless you get out of here in some days, or till your memory is back. If only I had told you about this book thing earlier you would've viewed it in other way. But now, you can either believe me or not but you can't go out and find out the truth for yourself unless you're fit to do so. And when you will, you'll laugh at yourself."

"The chapters written while I wasn't present there do not explain much. You might've easily mentioned the conversation to me anytime, there's no need for me to be physically there in order to be able to write it. You're really handling this well Karan. You're scared of them aren't you?" Vishal asked.

"Who's them? The fictional villains from the book!? My foot!" Karan spoke with a laugh.

"This isn't fun! I am totally confused and would be more than happy if your version of the story is true and this is just a fiction." Vishal had calmed down a bit now.

"Of course what I'm saying is true man! Can you believe it? A smuggling racket within a spiritual organization which teaches disciples not only in our country but internationally? You think it's so easy? Such things happen only in movies and books dude! I'm sorry but grow up and stop believing in fantasy!"

Vishal didn't say a word. Karan then bent forward as he placed his hands on Vishals' shoulder.

"Listen friend, you've just been out of a severe head injury, been in coma for a prolonged period of time, and to top it all you've lost your memory completely. Now you are constantly in search of your identity and trying to relate each and every thing to yourself. Your mind is playing games with you. Your ability to differentiate fact from fiction is up to its minimum. The doctor has advised me to not feed you with extra information about your past till you recover just so that you wouldn't think about it much and put less strain on yourself. I just hope you had read something else while I was away! Wasn't there a Superman comic lying around anywhere near you?" Karan joked in the end to lighten up the moment.

Vishal smiled. Now there was an awkward silence.

Neither Karan knew that whatever he had explained up till now was being believed by Vishal, nor did Vishal know whether to trust Karan or he was just trying to cover up the biggest secret of his own life. But Karan did make sense to Vishal partly even though in some minute corner of his brain and heart told him that Karan was hiding something. Or as Karan said, maybe it was just his quest for finding himself that he believed in his own written fiction story. It was weird. Weird for Vishal as well as Karan.

"And what about the nurse? She told me I wasn't in coma for 7 whole months as you informed me, she said she was told to 'shut up and do her work quietly' when asked about our accident!" Vishal asked.

"Dude", Karan began, "See these medicines tend to have a weird effect on you at times."

"You mean?"

"Hallucination.", Karan answered.

"Ridiculous!" Vishal shrieked, "Now you'll say the nurse here was imaginary too!?"

"No" Karan said, "She's for real, she gave you the laptop, told you things, but I guess you sub-consciously imagined some part of the conversation you had with her. Of course she wasn't given the information regarding the accident because it was a police case and the hospital authority wanted minimum staff involved. I have no clue why she had to tell you this with all the added drama and fantasy-made story about us trying to cover up something! Also, the reason why we told you that you were in coma since the accident for 7 whole months, was just to avoid further detailed information for your benefit so that you didn't think much, leading to more pressure on your brain. I can call the nurse right now and sort it out."

Vishal nodded in negative.

"So tell me where Richa is." Vishal spoke up after a minute, "Did she come here to visit me?"

"As I said, she's in Delhi, safe and sound. Yes, she did visit here, twice. The last time she visited was last month when you were in coma. Also the first time she had visited she was thrilled by the idea of our book! She even gave us permission to use her real name in it! The name of the camp, *A Way Around*, we had decided to change later and kept the teacher names also the same so that we related to the facts ourselves while writing the book. Once, were finished with it, we will be changing all of the details such as organization name and some other names as we don't want to fall into some legal battles for using their names for our fiction."

"Also Karan, there's a mention of a secret box given by her to me in the book. Was that for real or that was fictionalized too?"

"No, that part was real. The only thing we added for the fiction sake was that she has placed a chit and all in it with a number. The box was given to you as a gift by her, but the fact that it holds some kind of secret was totally made up. It was an empty box."

"Can I see that?"

"Of course." Karan said as he bent down to pull out a small palm sized cardboard box from below the hospital bed. From the box he drew out a plastic bag which had a mobile, a wallet and the 'secret box' given by Richa.

Vishal took the secret-box into his hand.

"It's locked." he said.

"Yes, probably you locked it while playing with it when you were here." Karan said.

Vishal then took the box next to his ear and shook it.

"It's making noise! There's something inside! There's a chit with the number which I was supposed to call when I thought it was my last option and didn't know what to do! You said she gave it to me as a present and it was empty!" Vishal again went back to his theory of believing that all that was written was indeed the truth than whatever Karan told him.

Karan laughed at Vishals' excitement.

"You know what Vishal? You just want to believe your version of the story and nothing else. I did tell you that when she gave it to you it was empty, why would I lie? Also, if we wanted to hide anything from you I would have answered you that even the box was a part of the story and not real! Why did I present it to you? Also, in the end the book suggests that our wallets, mobile and other belongings were confiscated by Kaushals' bodyguards so how come I have them here now?" Karan said pointing at the wallet and mobile of Vishal.

"How do I know this is my mobile and wallet, I don't remember a shit! These could belong to anyone!"

Karan clapped his hands together, "You mean we planted this too? To make you believe our version of the story? Ridiculous."

Vishal soon agreed that Karan did make sense.

"But then there's something in here" Vishal said again now in a calmer voice shaking the box.

"Yes, she did give it to you empty, but as I said you were often playing with it lying here. I'm pretty sure you've put something in there while playing with it and locked it with some code." Karan said pointing to the box.

"I understand." Vishal said, "But somehow now this box is the answer to all my questions."

"And how is that?"

"If whatever written in that book did happen for real, according to me, this box contains the chit inside it with the phone number that Richa had asked me to dial if anything went wrong or I reached a dead end. If your version of story is true and I have placed something in it while just fiddling with it, then there might be just some crap-chit or something that I already know or belongs to me."

"Right." Karan nodded, "Now but there's a catch. You obviously don't know the code that you had set for it don't you?"

"Yes, Karan. I don't know my own set code for the box. *IF* at all it was set by me here in the hospital and not by Richa in the camp." Vishal responded.

"This is it Vishal, now more than you, I pray that you finally manage to open up the box as it's the only thing that will make you entirely believe that I am right." Karan left the room.

Vishal instantly felt even sadder. He had no code. Even if Richa had given the secret box with the code set by her, as per the story, he didn't know the code. Also if Karan was to be believed and Vishal himself had set the code before slipping into the coma post-operation, he had forgotten it completely.

It was a difficult situation.

CHAPTER THIRTY SIX

It was 11p.m now. Karan had gone down to the first floor of the hospital to get the required medicines and injections as prescribed by the doctor for Vishal.

Vishal sat on his bed staring at the box, and then at the cell-phone. The cell-phone was on charging-mode for the last three hours and now it was fully charged. Vishal now un-plugged it from the charger and started it. He went through the contact list. Not a single contact rang a bell in his memory lane. Then something struck him. He went through the contact list again. He pressed down the scroll-key down till the alphabet 'R' appeared. He found out a contact named Richa in his phone. And then he dialed.

After eight rings Richa picked up the call.

"Hi Richa , it's me." Vishal said.

"Oh my goodness! You're okay! Finally!" she said

"Yes, I'm fine."

"I'm coming to see you this week now! I'm so happy for you!" she couldn't say anything further, she had started crying now.

"Why are you crying? I'm out of coma!" Vishal said

"You won't understand *dumbo*, I'm crying because I am happy! You're back. You saved me from those goons. Because of me you are there, in such a situation. I had visited you back then when you were working on your book. So wonderfully you had scripted those chapters where in we had first been out from the camp. And then I had helped you with some parts of it. Then all of a sudden you went into coma and I feared I would never see you normal again. I couldn't see the sight of you being a 'living' dead body. So I returned here. But now I can't wait for you to get alright and complete your dream now. I can't wait to see you. I can't wait to talk to you and I can't wait to hug you." She cried a little more.

Vishal listened patiently. He wished if only he could hug his crush right through the phone. But he cursed his fate as he had even forgotten how she looked. But going by the description in his book, he guessed she must be a beauty.

Vishal also noticed that every word that Karan had told him was true. Richa had indeed been here twice, had known about the 'novel' he was working on, and nothing seemed abnormal. He was again inclined towards Karan's version of the story.

"So tell me about that secret box that you gave me." Vishal asked

"What about that?"

"Why did you give it to me?"

"Just as a memoir of our lovely little friendship. Why do you ask?"

"Nothing, it's just that it's locked and you didn't tell me the code back then. How do I open and see what's inside?"

Richa paused for a moment, confused and then replied, "I had given it to you empty. The box had nothing in it. In the beginning the default code is ABCDE. But in case you've placed something in it and changed the code, I don't know."

"No, there IS something there. Have you set it with some secret in it and given it to me?" Vishal prompted

"No. You must've put it in yourself." Richa replied.

"Sure?"

There was a pause from Richa's side.

"Yes. Sure." she said after taking her own time.

"Okay, is there any other way to open it?"

"No, if you break it, the acid inside will burn out the paper or the information inside. Remember *Da-Vinci Code*?" Richa said.

Vishal nodded giving a silent 'yes' to her. She understood. They talked for about 15 minutes more. She again jumped with joy and promised Vishal to come over to the hospital in the coming weekend. They wished each other goodnight and then Vishal disconnected the phone.

'So whatever Karan told me regarding the box is also true.' Vishal thought, 'Am I really thinking a bit too much into the weird possibility that the book and the events in the documents might be true and Karan is trying to cover them up to avoid further risk? Everything that Karan told me is confirmed by Richa on the phone too. Is she involved in the cover up too? There's no way to know other than this box' Vishals' thought started to race again.

He couldn't believe his situation was in such a state right now. He didn't know what his own history was. Was it what his best friend and the girl on whom he had a crush told him? Or what he had written was the truth which was conveniently being brushed under the carpet taking advantage of his memory loss?

He stared at the box again.

He then tried the default code. A-B-C-D-E. The box didn't open.

This meant that he or Richa, HAD set the code.

He stared at it again.

'If only stares could open locks' He thought, 'Maybe I'm really a *dumbo*. And Karan's right. Maybe this all is just a fiction.'

Then suddenly just like a bolt of lightning, something struck his mind. He had read his 'book' in the afternoon. There was a word that was being mentioned quite regularly by Richa, *dumbo*.

She also said quite a few times, *"One day, you will like this word."*

According to his book, she had also mentioned that Vishal already knew the password to the box but didn't know that it was a password!

He picked up the box and checked the alphabetical dials, he started arranging them now.

D-U-M-B-O

'Perfect' he thought, '5 dials, and a 5 letter word that he knew and Richa claimed that he would like one day.'

He then adjusted all the five dials to align them in row. Now all he had to do was press the release button. If it were the right password the box would open revealing the secret inside.

He took a deep breath and pressed the release button with his index finger. There was a 'click' sound and within a flash, the box opened.

EPILOGUE

"Hey so you managed to open it!" Karan spoke as he noticed the open box beside Vishals' bed.

"Yes."

"So tell me, what is it?"

"A number, that Richa gave me."

"Richa gave you? Or you yourself had put it in there? How are you so sure?"

"It's written in the book."

"Oh God, so you're still stuck on to that theory aren't you? Anyways, did you dial and check who it belongs to?"

"Not yet."

"Why not?"

"I was waiting for you to come. You will dial it, we'll find out the truth, together."

Karan shrugged. But then extended his hand to take the chit of paper from Vishal. Karan then reached his pocket to pull out his cell phone. He then typed the number on the mobile screen and something struck him.

"Vishal, do you really want me to dial this number?" he asked.

"Of course yes. Why do you ask?" Vishal said.

"What do you expect will happen after I dial it?" Karan asked as he smiled.

"Why are you smiling? This number is the key to everything I need to know. Richa had said to me, whenever I'm at a dead end, 'HE' will be the one with all the answers. 'HE' will help me with all I need!"

"So you believe 'him' don't you?"

"Stop freaking me out Karan, Just-dial-the-number!"

Karan then pressed the dial button.

About for first 3 seconds nothing happened. And then, all of a sudden the phone beside Vishal that was kept for charging began to vibrate.

"What the –." Vishal was surprised, "Whose phone is that! Why is it ringing on dialing the number? Who left it here?"

Karan disconnected the call, came forward calmly, and placed his hand on Vishals' shoulders as he spoke, "My friend, this is the truth. Richa never placed the chit with any magic number in it. You must've done it yourself, and that itself is the truth I've been telling you all this time! That number is yours. Why would she place your number in the secrete box and give it to you?"

A cold shiver ran through Vishal's spine and he instantly began to sweat. He had hoped that this box would lead to the answers he'd been looking for all this time, and he'd got one. The number inside the box made a connection to the phone beside him. It started ringing on the dialing the number, it belonged to Vishal himself.

He also remembered the conversation he apparently had with Richa in the lodge about how she had told him that the box was nothing but a 'motivation factor' for him to make him relaxed thinking that there was a backup plan if anything went wrong. Well but even if the box was a prank perfectly played by Richa for Vishal's false hope, motivational purpose, now it had the number which belonged to Vishal himself!

Was it her way of telling Vishal that in crisis the only person we must trust and look forward to is ourselves? Maybe. But how did this prove any of the versions of the story right even now?

Vishal's own theory about the book? Or Karan's version of the story of it being a fictionalized factual account?

All this time he was thinking of ways to track the truth, but as his own book said, the path to discovery does not always go around with us to guide us.

At times, it's *the other way round.*

www.ingramcontent.com/pod-product-compliance
Lightning Source LLC
Chambersburg PA
CBHW052030020726
47501CB00004B/1343